"Good morning," he greeted unexpectedly. *"Beautiful day, isn't it?"* Alex added in a deep male voice, but she had an idea he wasn't just commenting on the weather.

At the way his sensual gaze swept over her in frank male pleasure, a wave of heat consumed her. The breath seemed to catch in her lungs. She almost dropped the nozzle.

"I-It's lovely out," she stammered, like a love-struck teenager instead of a twenty-four-year-old widow.

On legs weak as jelly, she rushed inside to pay for the fuel. By the time she'd returned, his car was halfway down the street, leaving her with an achy sensation that made no sense at all.

Gilly hadn't thought there was a man who could make her feel that inexplicably breathless kind of wanting again.

Father by Choice **is set in the evocative and beautiful setting of Yellowstone National Park. We asked Rebecca, where is the most romantic place you've ever traveled?**

"The most romantic place I've ever been to is an area near Vevey, Switzerland, on Lake Geneva. With the French Alps on one side, and the Jura mountains on the Swiss side, you begin your climb through thriving vineyards, the greenest green meadows, past pines and quaint brown-and-white chalets to fields of wild narcissus blossoming in riotous color.

Far below you stands the Château de Chillon, a magnificent medieval castle. The combination of serene blue water, perfumed air, exquisite mountain scenery and the distant sound of the alpenhorn leads you to believe you have found paradise on earth.

With your lover, a picnic basket, a warm sun and glorious nature, you'll think you've died and gone to heaven."

FATHER BY CHOICE

Rebecca Winters

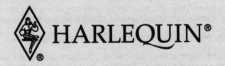

TORONTO • NEW YORK • LONDON
AMSTERDAM • PARIS • SYDNEY • HAMBURG
STOCKHOLM • ATHENS • TOKYO • MILAN • MADRID
PRAGUE • WARSAW • BUDAPEST • AUCKLAND

ISBN 0-373-18226-0

FATHER BY CHOICE

First North American Publication 2006.

www.eHarlequin.com

Printed in U.S.A.

Rebecca Winters, whose family of four children has now swelled to include three beautiful grandchildren, lives in Salt Lake City, Utah, in the land of the Rocky Mountains. With canyons and high Alpine meadows full of wildflowers, she never runs out of places to explore, and they—along with her favorite vacation spots in Europe—often end up as backgrounds for her Harlequin Romance® novels. Writing is her passion, along with her family and church. Rebecca loves to hear from her readers. If you wish to e-mail her, please visit her Web site at www.rebeccawinters-author.com

For previous books by Rebecca Winters visit www.eHarlequin.com

CHAPTER ONE

"THIS is the new acrylic-lined linen paper I was telling you about, Gilly. It just came in. Have you ever seen such a beautiful surface? The panels are slightly rough, just enough to grab the paint, but it's a fine weave."

Gilly King held one up to the light. "The paper's perfect. I'll buy the packet."

"Can I get you any paints?"

"Not today, thanks." She'd been ordering Brera acrylics from Italy online. They had that true Hooker's green for landscapes she couldn't seem to find anywhere else.

"Very good. Then I'll ring you up."

A seven-by-seven-inch ceramic frame caught her eye. It would be ideal for the gift she planned to make for her mother's birthday which wasn't far off. She handed it to the clerk.

Within a few minutes Gilly left the art supply store in Gardiner, Montana, with her purchases and headed for her car parked in front of Willard's Book Emporium. On impulse she went inside to buy a couple of thrillers and a newspaper.

The huge grandfather clock which had survived the Hebgen Lake earthquake years earlier chimed the quarter. She glanced over at it: 10:15 a.m. If she hurried, she'd have the rest of her day off to get busy on her latest project.

There was an area near Yellowstone Lake with a meadow of wildflowers that had just come into bloom. Now would be the time to capture them on canvas.

Before Gilly drove back to Yellowstone Park through the North Entrance, she noticed she was low on gas. Might as well fill the tank while she was here. But to her dismay there were lots of cars waiting to use the pumps everywhere she looked. Still, the crowds were worse in the park where there weren't as many gas stations.

She spied Grandy's convenience store on the corner and got in line to wait her turn. It was going to be a while. While she sat there, she read the paper.

Every so often she moved her car. Finally she was able to pull up to the rear pump and get out to fill the tank. That's when her attention was distracted by a man with a burnished complexion who looked to be in his midthirties. He'd alighted from a blue Ford Explorer in front of her to wash his windshield.

His dark blond hair was short cropped. Some of the top strands were naturally sun bleached, reminding her of guys who spent their summers surfing.

He might be dressed in a T-shirt and jeans typical of so many of the tourists, but his well-honed physique caused her to stare. Like her brothers, he stood tall, at least six-two.

Gilly studied his hard boned features, focusing for a moment on his wide mouth. Its sensual male curve seemed to snake right through to her insides, making them quiver.

To experience a strong physical response like this came as a total surprise to Gilly. Two years ago she'd lost her husband, and hadn't been able to look at another man since.

His car had Washington license plates. Was he on vacation? If he'd come through the park and had been in one of her groups, she would have definitely remembered. As far as a man's looks went, his were unforgettable.

While she found herself wondering about the color of his eyes beneath those well-formed brows, he happened to glance up at her. His eyes flashed molten-silver and Gilly's body trembled from their deep penetration.

"Good morning," came his unexpected greeting. "Beautiful day, isn't it?" he added in a deep male voice, but she had an idea he wasn't just commenting on the weather.

At the way his sensual gaze swept over her in frank male pleasure, a wave of heat consumed her. The breath seemed to catch in her lungs. She almost dropped the nozzle.

"I-It's lovely out," she stammered like a love-struck teenager instead of a twenty-four-year-old widow.

On legs weak as jelly, she rushed inside to pay for the gas. By the time she'd returned to her car, the Explorer was halfway down the street, leaving her with an achy sensation that made no sense at all. In seconds the disturbing stranger would vanish from sight.

Gilly hadn't thought there was a man who could make her feel that inexplicably breathless kind of wanting again.

Not only was she shocked by her feelings— it seemed such a terrible betrayal of Kenny's memory.

Her funny, cute, wonderful, darling Kenny. The boy she'd loved since second grade. The guy she'd married out of high school. The father of their stillborn baby. Her rock who'd helped her to believe there would be more babies in time.

His death had been her point of reference for life. The day before he'd died it had been the end of May and her heart had been alive. But the next day, when he would have been with their families at the commencement exercises to watch her graduate from college, he'd been killed on the freeway by a drunk driver who'd veered into his lane.

Overcome by grief from both losses, the rest of that year had been a blur for Gilly. What made things even more difficult was her perception of herself as "different" from her over-achiever family.

Gilly had been the baby of the highly educated Bryson clan. Her dad was still chancellor at the University of California in San Diego, her mom was a city court judge, her oldest brother Trevor was an attorney in a big name law firm, and her next oldest brother Wade had just graduated from medical school.

But Gilly wasn't like them. Without Kenny in her future, she hadn't known where to turn, what to do with her life. She'd thought they'd raise a family and be together forever. Her future had been shattered.

Though she'd obtained a communications degree, she'd planned to try for another baby and be a stay-at-home mom. Kenny worked for his father and made a wonderful living for them so she wouldn't have to work.

Completely lost, Gilly's mother had been the one to suggest she take a test to determine what career she was suited for where her degree could be of help.

When Gilly saw the answers, it was a revelation to discover they all had to do with the outdoors. Yet it wasn't surprising really. She and Kenny had spent their lives enjoying water sports and sailing. Anything to do with the ocean and nature.

After looking over the list, the only thing that halfway interested her was the idea of becoming a park ranger where she could be outside on a daily basis. Her parents encouraged her to investigate, hinting it was time she made the physical and emotional break from Kenny's family and all the attendant associations of him and the baby in order to heal.

In the fall she left for Montana to apply for work with the National Park Service. Though everyone in her family felt it was the healthy thing to do, Kenny's family begged her not to go. From the time she'd been a young woman, they'd loved her like a daughter. They'd mourned the loss of the baby and their son. If she went away, it would be like they'd lost everyone dear to them.

Without her own family urging her to reach out for a new life, Gilly wouldn't have been able to find the courage to leave. When she accepted her first assignment at Teton National Park, she'd been afraid to tell Kenny's parents. She finally did, but they'd made her feel terrible about her choices.

Living with the constant guilt of disappointing his family, coupled with the painful loss of her husband and child, Gilly's last two years had been difficult. In order to get through them, she'd poured all her energy into her career as a ranger.

Though there'd been plenty of opportunities to meet men, whether they were rangers or guys employed in the nearby towns, or even tourists just passing through, she'd been oblivious.

Until now…

The mere thought of the striking male who'd made her aware of her femininity to the very core of her being caused her heart to turn over. But this unwanted, unexpected reaction filled her with fresh guilt.

At Kenny's funeral she'd sworn to love him forever.

* * *

If Alex Latimer didn't have an important meeting at the chief ranger's office, he would have stayed to talk to the shapely female in the pale blue top and designer jeans just getting back in her red Toyota.

She had beautiful hair, a rich brown that glistened in the warm sun. He liked the way it was cut just below the jawline. He liked everything about her from her brilliant blue eyes and heart-shaped mouth to her small, cute feet wearing expensive-looking Italian leather sandals.

The woman painted her nails and toenails. He liked that, too. She looked expensive and well cared for. Her car was immaculate. So was she.

It had been a long time since he'd felt such a strong, instant, physical attraction to a woman who was probably ten to twelve years younger than himself.

Thirty-four wasn't exactly old, but he drew the line at getting involved with anyone too much younger than himself. Maybe she was older. With some women, age was hard to tell.

It had been a while since he'd had an intimate relationship with a woman, the latest being over a year ago. Since then he'd dated some, but the desire for anything more hadn't been there.

Lately he'd wondered if something was

wrong with him. But the fact that he'd noted the woman's Wyoming license plate number while she'd been inside the store meant he was still vulnerable if and when the right female got fixed in his sights.

Maybe she was from the Jackson area. When he had the time to speak to Larry, the ranger in charge of park security, he'd ask the other man to look up the information on her. Depending on her age, Alex might try to accidentally bump into her another time and go from there.

Before long he pulled the car into the parking area at Park Headquarters in Mammoth. If tourists hadn't exploded on the scene in the last week with their trailers, kayaks and fishing boats, he would have accomplished the short trip from Gardiner even faster. But his thoughts had been so full of the stunning brunette, the heavy traffic hadn't bothered him.

Striding through the milling crowds, he made his way inside the building past reception to Jim Archer's office. His secretary told him to go on in. "Quinn Derek just got here."

"Thanks, Roberta."

When he entered the room, both men stood up.

"Quinn? Jim?" He shook hands with them before sitting down in front of Jim's desk.

Quinn followed suit. "Thanks for getting here so fast, Alex. The governor of the State has asked me to do him a personal favor and talk to you." He wore an expectant expression.

Personal? That wasn't what Alex had been expecting. It didn't sound too ominous. In fact put like that he could hardly refuse the park superintendent. They'd been good friends long before Alex had become the chief ranger of volcanology at Yellowstone a month ago.

"Name it."

Quinn's eyes lit up in amusement. "Don't be so quick to say yes. I can tell you right now this is the last thing any ranger would want to do, but you're the only man both of us could think of who's perfect for the job. You're the ideal role model."

Role model— "For what?"

"Before I answer that question, let me assure you it would only be for a month."

Alex grunted. "Starting when?"

"Day after tomorrow."

Jim Archer was sitting back in his chair, grinning. What in the devil?

"How would you like to let a teenager shadow you in your job?"

The surprising question caused him to rub his thumb absently against his lower lip. "If you when no one else would. The man's work ethic had ignited something in Alex. It had been the beginning of his road out of hell.

"I appreciate your faith in me, Quinn." He studied the other man for a moment. "I'm willing to give it a try."

Quinn looked slightly surprised Alex had made the decision so fast. "That's wonderful. I'm indebted to you," he said in a heartfelt tone. "If this works, it could be the beginning of a permanent program."

"What about the apartment I'm sharing with Bruce? He'll have to be in agreement, too. We're cramped for space as it is."

"Don't worry about that," Jim interjected. "As I told you when you first arrived, that was only temporary. The furnished house at Grant Village I earmarked for you is now vacant. The repairs on it have been done, so it's ready to move into. You and Jamal will have the place to yourselves. Divide your time between West Thumb and Norris as you see fit. Whatever works best for you."

He reached in the drawer and handed him a set of keys. "It's number ten. Take the rest of today and tomorrow off to get settled. The teen will be arriving at West Yellowstone airport on Thursday at 3:00 p.m. He'll probably want to get settled in with you first, so bring him to headquarters on Friday and we'll introduce him around."

"That sounds like a plan."

"Alex—" Quinn looked concerned. "The boy has to live up to certain standards of behavior. If he can't obey your rules, then he'll be sent back home. Call Jim or me if you can see the situation isn't working. Since we haven't tried this before, you'll be breaking new ground here. For Jamal's sake, let's hope he lasts long enough to get something out of the program."

Jim eyed Alex soberly. "If he can't learn from you, then it means he's too far gone. I hope that's not the case. In any event, we can't allow this to interfere with your work. Anytime you want to call it quits, we'll know you gave it your all."

For the sake of the teen, Alex *would* give it his all. But it would probably be too little, too late. Like seventeen years… No doubt the grocer had felt exactly the same way about Alex when he'd been coerced into hiring him by the social worker.

"Fair enough." He got to his feet.

Quinn shook his hand again. "We were lucky to get the top man away from Mount Rainier into our camp. If this private experiment works,

"How come this place is called West Thumb?" a boy asked Gilly. He sounded like he was from the Deep South of the U.S.

"That's because Yellowstone Lake looks like a hand with a thumb and fingers."

"Are there really wolves around here?" his little sister asked. She had to be about six years old. Gilly's own little girl would be about that age right now if she'd lived....

"Yes, honey. The black and gray wolves of the Soda Butte Pack are found in the southern half of Yellowstone Park. It ranges from Heart Lake on the west, to the east shore of Yellowstone Lake on the east and the headwaters of the Yellowstone River on the south."

"Ooh." She shivered.

Their father raised his hand. "How big is the park?"

"It covers 2.2 million acres."

"I had no idea of its size."

A ripple of surprise sounded from the large crowd assembled. It was the sixth of June already, the beginning of high season. Schools were out across the nation. To Gilly, it felt like most families had chosen the park to begin their summer vacation.

A week ago she'd been living in Mammoth at the northwest end of the park where she'd worked the last nine months. Then the assignment she'd wanted had come through.

She'd quickly moved out of the cabin she'd been sharing with Beth Hayes, another ranger. Now she lived in a house that had just been repaired in the Grant Village area. So far she had it all to herself.

For the last few days the park had been flooded with tourists. Since 9:00 a.m. she'd already given four lectures to groups from fifty to a hundred people each. This was her last before she went off duty at 4:00 p.m.

Unfortunately she hadn't noticed the construction worker who'd joined this lecture until it was too late. If she'd realized, she would have asked one of the rangers manning the West Thumb Information Center to fill in for her this time around.

A construction crew from Bozeman, Montana, had been busy all week repairing roofs, chimneys and porches. The heavy winter snowfall always did some damage to the rangers' houses.

This guy had been working on the house next to Gilly's. Because part of the roof had fallen in, one of the married rangers and his wife had been forced to move to housing at the other end of the park, leaving it vacant for the next ranger to move into once the repairs were done.

Every time Gilly came or went from her house, she saw the guy up on a ladder or some such thing. He never missed an opportunity to flirt with her. A few days ago he'd asked her out. She'd refused. This morning he'd been at her again. She'd ignored him. But his appearance here meant he wasn't about to take no for an answer.

She led her tour group back to the Information Center, signaling the lecture was over. Everyone thanked her and got in their cars except for the construction worker.

It gave her the creeps the way he stood there staring at her. "You're good at what you do. Mind if I ask you something?"

"Actually, I do." She started to walk away. He caught up to her.

"Why won't you go out with me? Do I have two heads or something?"

She'd had it! "Why isn't 'no' enough for you?"

"Because I can't resist you in that ranger's outfit."

At this point there was only one way to deal with him. "Come near me or talk to me again and I'll report you to Chief Ranger Archer."

Jim would take care of the problem for her in a big hurry.

Hoping her threat produced the desired results, she walked toward her government issue truck and got in. After leaving the parking area, she headed for the house to change out of uniform. Then she'd drive her Toyota into West Yellowstone, the town outside the West Entrance to the park.

The Levi's jacket she'd ordered from Blythe's Sporting Goods store had come in. Now would be a good time to pick it up. She didn't want to dwell on the unpleasant incident.

It might not be fair to put that creepy guy in the same category as David Cracroft, the ranger who'd stalked her to the point she'd had to transfer from Teton Park to the Yellowstone Mammoth area last fall. But she wasn't taking any chances.

If this guy was anywhere around Grant Village when she returned from town, she'd phone security for help.

Alex glanced at the teen he'd just picked up at the airport. Jamal Carter had to be about five feet ten. Between his baseball cap which he wore backward, plus his baggy pants and long sleeved shirt, he'd been impossible to miss.

"Tell you what, Jamal. Since you've had two airplane rides in one day, what do you say we go home and kick back until tomorrow."

"That's cool."

The teen had to be nervous, but no more so than Alex

"First however, let's buy you some jeans and T-shirts. What you're wearing was fine for school, but it's summer now and it gets hot at this elevation. You'll be more comfortable dressed like me."

"How high is it?"

"Anywhere from 5,200 to 11,000 feet, depending on where you are at a given moment." The boy whistled. "Coming from sea level you'll probably notice yourself breathing a little harder until your lungs adapt."

"Yeah. I feel kind of weird."

Alex couldn't help but admire Jamal for his courage. That's what it took to come to a strange place, away from everything familiar.

He started up the engine and they took off for the clothing store a couple of streets over. "I understand you've never flown before."

Jamal squinted at him. "You know I haven't, man—"

Alex would have hated being patronized, too, so it was time to change tactics.

"My name's Alex. I'd like you to use it. You'll call the other rangers Mr., Mrs. or Ms. unless they tell you otherwise.

"And let's get something else straight. You're lucky you've got a mom who loves you and wants the best for you. Though your father's in prison, you at least know who he is, and where he is, even if you hate his guts. I spent the first half of my life doing little else but hating.

"Then this grocer came along who taught me there was more to life than wishing I'd never been born. The only reason I agreed to let you shadow me is because it's the one way I know to pay that person back. In fact you're doing me a favor.

"As for you, whatever you make of this experience is your own business. You want to go home now, I'll put you on the next plane out of here. You don't play straight with me, and you'll be gone in a heartbeat. Understood?"

By now Jamal was staring straight ahead. "Yeah."

"Try saying 'yes'."

"Yes."

"Good. Now let's get you some new clothes."

While he looked for a parking place near Blythe's, the knockout woman he'd seen in

Gardiner the other day emerged from its doors carrying a package.

"She's gorgeous," Jamal commented.

Alex knew exactly whom the teen was referring to. There was nothing wrong with his eyesight. Jamal craned his neck out the open window to watch her progress the way Alex wanted to do. *And couldn't!*

The next thing he knew, Jamal let out a whistle the whole street could hear.

"Jamal!"

"Sorry," he muttered as the startled brunette turned to look in their direction. For a breathless moment her shocked gaze met Alex's. While he drank his fill at the appealing sight of her, he almost rammed the car in front of him and had to slam on the brakes.

Jamal made a whoop of laughter.

After letting out a curse, Alex tried to see where she was headed, but she moved fast. Too fast! Damn if he wasn't going in the wrong direction and couldn't back up or make a U-turn in the traffic.

She had to be on vacation and had probably traveled down through the park from Mammoth. For all he knew she'd visited the Norris Geyser Basin where he worked. Naturally it had to be the one time when he'd been absent from his job in order to get the house ready for him and Jamal.

Eventually he found a parking spot around the corner. By now his mystery woman had long since disappeared, but he had an idea. The second they entered the store, Alex approached the nearest clerk and asked her to help outfit Jamal.

While the woman took Jamal in hand, Alex walked over to the counter where a male clerk was working. This one looked college aged.

"Hi! Can I help you?"

"I was wondering if you could tell me anything about the good-looking brunette woman with the blue eyes who just left the store carrying a package?"

The guy flashed him a wry smile. "All I know is that the item she picked up was for a G. King."

That was a start.

"Does she come in here often?"

"I don't know. I just started work for the summer."

He pulled a five out of his wallet and put it on the counter. "Thanks for the information."

"That's okay." The clerk handed it back to Alex. "May the best man win."

CHAPTER TWO

ALEX swore under his breath once more and wandered over by Jamal. Within twenty minutes they were on their way again with a wardrobe that included a new parka, gloves, boots, socks, sweats, underwear and a couple of flannel shirts and pajamas.

The female clerk had fussed over him. Though Jamal didn't say anything, Alex could tell he'd enjoyed the experience.

For that matter, Alex had enjoyed funding this buying spree. It was fun to watch Jamal stand in front of the floor-length mirror while he decided which clothes suited him best. Take that hat off, and get him to stand up straight and he was a nice-looking kid his mother would be proud of.

"We'll get some pictures of you in your new outfit so you can send them to your mom."

Jamal may have rolled his eyes, but he still nodded.

When they arrived at the West Entrance to the park, Alex asked the ranger he recognized to step out of the booth. Coming from the other end of the park, Alex still hadn't met all the rangers.

"Larry? I'd like you to meet Jamal Carter from Indianapolis."

The burly blonde walked around to the passenger side of the car and extended his hand with a smile. "Pleased to meet you, Jamal."

"He's out here for a month shadowing me in my job for his high school careers class," Alex explained. "Jamal? This is Ranger Larry Smith. He's the head of security, the chief ranger's right hand."

"Hi." Jamal kept his eyes averted.

"Welcome to the greatest park in the nation, Jamal. You're a fortunate young man to be working with Alex."

The teen was clearly uncomfortable.

"We've got a house in the Village," Alex informed him.

"Which one?"

"Number ten."

Larry's eyes lit up. "You lucky dog."

"What does that mean?"

"How long have you lived next to number eleven?"

"A day."

"That explains it."

"Explains what?"

"You'll find out," he teased before looking at Jamal. "Anything you need when he can't be around, call headquarters and they'll find me."

"Thanks, ma— Mr. Smith." Jamal amended. Alex was impressed.

"Call me Larry."

"Okay."

Alex gave Larry an appreciative nod before driving on. Who in the hell lived in number eleven?

Further along the highway a couple of the younger rangers who made regular patrols of the park spotted Alex's car. They slowed down in their truck to acknowledge him.

Even though it backed up traffic, he applied the brakes and made the introductions. The sooner everyone got acquainted with Jamal and knew he'd be living with Alex at the Village, the faster he would fit in, *if* he was going to.

They flashed Jamal friendly smiles. "You couldn't have been sent to a greater person to learn the business. In a few days when you're settled, we'll come to your house after we're off duty and show you around. What number?"

"Ten," Alex informed them.

The two rangers exchanged secretive glances. "You lucked out big time," they muttered. Another reference to Alex's neighbor. Obviously a female. "We'll definitely be by, Jamal."

"That'll be cool."

Alex started driving again. Perhaps the other two hadn't heard the boredom in Jamal's voice, but it prompted him to say, "Something's been eating at you since we left the store. Want to talk about it now or later?"

A troubled sigh escaped the teen's lips. "What am I doing here?" he blurted. "This isn't my scene." Jamal shook his head.

"Then make it yours," Alex challenged quietly. "It's a free country."

He turned off the highway toward the cluster of group housing for the rangers. A few seconds later and he pulled in to his driveway. There was no sign of life at number eleven, no cars visible.

Pressing the remote on the visor that opened the garage door, he drove in and parked next to his government truck.

"We're home, Jamal. Stick with me and you might like it so much, you'll decide to become a ranger."

Hilarious laughter resounded in the car.

"You're funny, man." He caught himself. "I mean, Alex."

Alex warmed to the boy who had to be feeling lost and apprehensive, yet was able to display an amusing sense of humor.

"Come on inside. It may only be a bungalow, but it'll look good to you at the end of a long day in the hot sun. We've got the best drinking water this side of the Continental Divide."

In fact out of all the places on the planet, this assignment at Yellowstone was where Alex desired to be on a permanent basis. He'd found a place that felt like home.

He got out of the car and reached for the sacks in the backseat. "Can you cook?"

Jamal blinked in the process of reaching for the duffel bag that served as a suitcase. "Like what?"

"Anything."

Alex heard him start to say yeah, then he quickly changed it to yes.

"That's a relief. We'll trade off fixing breakfast and dinner. I'll cook tonight. How do hamburgers sound?"

"Good," the teen answered, sounding in a kind of daze.

Alex had been in a daze since he'd looked into those gorgeous blue eyes again. In fact the last few days had been surreal to him in more ways than one and he just hoped the mystery brunette crossed his path again.

The next morning Gilly was just backing out of her garage in the truck to go to work when she heard a whistle float through her open window.

Gilly braked and turned her head to find out who'd called to her. There was no sign of the construction worker, thank heaven. But she received the shock of her life to discover it was the teenager with the baseball cap who'd whistled and waved to her last evening.

The one riding in the Explorer with the striking man who'd reduced her limbs to liquid twice in the last few days.

She still hadn't recovered.

At the moment the high school boy was changing the rear tire of a government truck parked in the next driveway. He'd turned on the radio. His head bobbed to rock music.

When she could gather her wits she called back to him. "Good morning! That's quite a whistle you've developed." He stood up with a grin. "What's your name?"

"Jamal Carter."

"Nice to meet you, Jamal. I'm Gilly King."

His smile widened. "The rangers were right about you."

"What do you mean?"

"They said we were lucky to be living next to number eleven."

"They said *that*?"

"Yes ma'am. I mean Ms. King."

She was Mrs. King, but he didn't know that. "Call me Gilly."

Her heart began to thud in her chest. Did this mean the incredibly handsome male whose image had made chaos of her emotions was her new neighbor?

No. It wasn't possible. She hadn't heard about anyone moving into the vacant house. Yet there was this teen, big as life.

"Was that your father I saw you with in the Explorer?"

The boy started to laugh. "No way," he responded, as if what she'd said had sounded outrageous to him. "I'm just living with him part of the summer."

Only rangers lived in these houses. That man was a *ranger*?

You're not supposed to be thinking about that man, Gilly.

"You mean here?" she blurted in shock. "I mean in *that* house?"

His smile slowly faded. "Yes," he murmured before getting back to his job as if she didn't exist.

After he'd been so friendly seconds ago, what had she said to make him close up like that and ignore her? Before she could ask him, he disappeared inside the garage. The door lowered.

Puzzled by his behavior, she had no choice but to leave for the Information Center. Though she always threw herself into her work, this was one day when she couldn't get her mind off her new neighbors.

By the time she was winding up her last lecture tour for the day, she was so eager to get home and find out what was going on, she could hardly concentrate.

"The West Thumb thermal features are found not only on the lake shore here, but extend under the surface of the lake as well. Several underwater geysers were discovered in the early 1990s.

"Now that it's summer, you'll notice they're like slick spots or slight bulges. But during the winter, the underwater thermal features are visible as melt holes in the icy surface of the lake."

"How thick does it get?"

Gilly glanced at the woman who'd asked the

question. "The ice averages about three feet—" She broke off talking because she'd just caught sight of a dark blond male who must have just joined the group in the last few minutes.

Tall and suntanned with those powerful shoulders covered by a khaki T-shirt, he couldn't be anyone but the man she'd seen driving Jamal. He was too far away for her to read his expression, but his mere presence sent an inexplicable tremor through her body.

"Is there any reason for alarm?" he spoke up unexpectedly.

She got the instant impression that the mysterious ranger had decided to put her on the spot. Why?

He'd spoken in a deep, commanding voice, as if they were the only two people around.

Attempting to compose herself she said, "No. It's important to understand that current geologic activity at Yellowstone has remained relatively constant since earth scientists first started monitoring some thirty years ago.

"Although another caldera-forming eruption is theoretically possible, it is very unlikely to occur for thousands of years.

"Since 1993, Global Positioning Systems have been stationed in various parts of the park. They detect changes in elevation and horizontal shifts of one inch or less per year, helping us understand the processes that drive Yellowstone's active volcanic and earthquake systems."

"How do they work?"

None of the tourists sensed what was going on, but Gilly received the distinct impression he was angry, deliberately putting her through some kind of test. She couldn't recall another ranger ever trying to intimidate her this way. Attractive as he was, he'd aroused her ire.

"These systems include a constellation of twenty-four satellites, launched and operated by the United States Air Force, which transmits radio signals. When used according to standardized procedures, GPS receivers can determine positional coordinates to centimeter-level accuracy anywhere on the surface of the Earth.

"At the current time they're monitoring underground volcanic activity here at Yellowstone, particularly the presence of a massive volcanic bulge forming on the bottom of the lake. Though smaller eruptions are more likely to occur, we see no signals of any impending volcanic unrest. Prospects of renewed volcanism are still far away, so you don't need to worry."

"That's reassuring," he drawled without the slightest trace of humor, though others in the crowd chuckled.

Her jaw hardened. She looked around. "Are there any other questions?"

"Yes." A young marine smiled at her. "What are you doing after work?"

More chuckles and a few whistles. There was always one in the crowd.

She flashed him a professional smile. "I've got a date with a bunch of bats that need clearing out from some of the latrines so you people can enjoy the park."

That produced a spate of laughter from everyone except the unsmiling ranger.

"If that's all, then the lecture's over. Enjoy your visit to the park."

Once the crowd dispersed, Gilly wasn't surprised that the ranger approached her. His eyes glittered like her mom's set of sterling silver, raking her over with one dismissive glance. It was quite a change from the way he'd looked at her at the gas pump.

Going on the offensive she said, "Did I pass?"

He stood there with his hands on his hips in an aggressively male stance. Not even Kenny had this blatant kind of masculine appeal that got to her in spite of his hostile treatment of her.

"Your content and delivery get A plus. But a ranger needs other skills."

"Which I appear to lack in your eyes. Why don't we start over. I'm Gilly King. And you are…"

"Alex Latimer."

She moaned inwardly. Dr. Alex Latimer. "I recognize the name," she managed to say in an amazingly calm voice. "You're the prize the superintendent stole from Mount Rainier last month and installed at Norris."

A bleak expression crossed over his arresting features. "Tell me something, Ranger King. Does your prejudice extend to most minorities, or only to someone like Jamal who's come all the way from Indianapolis?"

Good grief.

Gilly had to believe the reputed scientist was normally a civilized man who didn't go around purposely insulting his colleagues without a very good reason.

Her thoughts flicked back to her meeting with Jamal. For the life of her she couldn't figure out what she'd done.

"It's clear Jamal believes I snubbed him in some way, otherwise you wouldn't be coming on as strong as a mother bear protecting her cub."

That mouth she'd been drawn to curved without mirth. "Interesting analogy."

This was getting them nowhere. "Mind telling me exactly what he said I said or did that gave him that impression?"

He sucked in his breath. "For starters, how about displaying your revulsion that he was going to be your next door neighbor."

Her dark, finely arched brows knit together in a frown. She reflected back to her conversation with the boy before he'd abruptly turned away from her.

Was that your father I saw you with yesterday?

No way. I'm just living with him part of the summer.

You mean here? I mean in that house?

Yes.

A moan escaped her throat, one Ranger Latimer heard or his lips wouldn't have tightened.

Jamal had totally misinterpreted her reaction. But if she told this man the truth, that since she'd seen him in Gardiner a few days ago and hadn't been able to get him out of her mind, then he would know her guilty secret. It was one she'd rather take to her grave than share with him.

"Where's Jamal right now?"

"Home cooking dinner."

"That's where I'm headed. If you don't mind, I'd like to clear up the misunderstanding in person. This is between him and me."

For a breathless moment he studied her through veiled eyes. "Be my guest."

So the man wasn't completely devoid of reason where she was concerned. But close.

"Tell Jamal I'll be over in a few minutes."

She walked to her truck without looking back and took off for the Village.

He wasn't far behind in his truck. They ended up turning in to their driveways at the same time. While Alex parked in the garage, she climbed down from the cab and marched straight across to the front porch of the other house.

Jamal appeared at the door after she knocked. He looked surprised and not at all happy to see her.

"Hi, Jamal. We need to talk about what happened this morning. Can you leave the dinner you're cooking long enough to come outside where we can speak alone?"

He wore a mutinous expression. "What's there to talk about?"

"Plenty."

"Alex told you, didn't he."

"Yes, and I'm glad, otherwise you and I would be enemies forever for no good reason."

That seemed to startle him, but he still didn't budge.

No doubt Ranger Latimer was lurking somewhere in the background, taking in every word. So be it.

"Tell me something first, Jamal. When you arrived at this house yesterday, did you see a construction worker up on the roof?"

He stared at her. "Yes, but he was just leaving and drove away in his truck."

"Well, for the last week that guy has been hounding me to go out on a date with him. I told him no, but he's the kind of man who doesn't care what a woman wants or doesn't want. When he showed up at my lecture the other day and asked me out again, I made a decision. If he tried to hang around me anymore, I'd have to report him to Chief Ranger Archer."

Jamal's eyes widened. "I met him today."

"He's a good man. You see I used to work at Teton National Park. In fact I was there a little over a year when all of a sudden a ranger began stalking me.

"It got so bad that Chief Ranger Gallagher had me transferred to Yellowstone Park."

"No way!"

"It's a long story and a bad one, Jamal. So when I saw you in the driveway this morning, and found out you and one of the rangers had moved in without my being aware of it, you have no idea how happy I was. I couldn't believe another ranger had taken up residence so quickly. What you heard was my excitement, *not* my bias.

"The problem was, I was late for work. And you went inside the garage before I could explain that as long as the house remained empty, I was frightened that the construction worker would find some excuse to keep pestering me.

"Because our two houses are on the end here, we're a little isolated from the others. But your presence has solved all my problems. I'm so thrilled you're here to protect me, you have no idea."

On impulse she hugged him. By the time she'd released him, a smile had broken out on his cute face.

"I guess I had you figured wrong."

"I guess you did." She sobered. "Thanks for giving me a chance to explain. You remind me of…someone I used to know." She explained, thinking of Kenny. "He would get angry and hurt real fast, but he got over it real fast, too. That's what I loved about him.

"Whenever you get sick and tired of your own company, or Ranger Latimer's," she said in a voice loud enough to penetrate the house, "come on over. I make yummy doughnuts." She started to leave.

"How about tomorrow?" he called to her.

"Perfect. I'll be home by four-thirty."

"Can Alex come, too?"

"Nope. No rangers allowed."

His amused laughter followed her all the way into her house.

Alex watched Jamal shut the door. The teen turned to him. "Did you hear that?"

"How could I not?"

"She said you weren't invited. You must have made her mad."

"I suppose I did."

In fact there was no supposing about it. He'd given her a hard time in front of the tourists, but she'd handled it like a pro. There was no excuse for what he'd done. He'd totally misjudged her.

The problem was, his physical attraction to her had been so strong, he couldn't handle being disappointed in her character. It had caused him to overreact in a way she wasn't about to forgive anytime soon.

"How long do you think it will take her to get over it?" Jamal had a way of reading his mind.

"I don't know. It could take a long time. Come on. Let's eat."

Jamal had warmed up canned spaghetti, but he'd made buttered toast and sprinkled garlic salt on it.

"This tastes good," he complimented Jamal a few minutes later. Luckily they'd eaten a big lunch with Jim at Mammoth so neither of them was starving.

On the way back to Grant Village, he'd let Jamal drive the truck to see how well he handled it. The boy had to be cautioned about staying within the park's forty-five mile an hour speed limit, but other than that he was a good driver.

He ought to be after the years he and his friends had probably eluded the cops around his old neighborhood. Alex had stolen cars in his early teens by hot-wiring them. Jamal wouldn't have been any different.

"Tell you what," Alex said after they'd finished. "While I do the dishes, you can take the truck for an hour. Get it filled at the gas station first. Tell them to charge it to my account." Alex handed him the keys, hoping Jamal would repay his trust.

That was Jamal's first real grin. Cars and girls were the way to his heart. Alex decided it was a good sign the boy wasn't hard-core yet.

"Don't worry. I won't crash it."

"I'm a lot more worried about the girls you'll be checking out. Just see that's all you do. From a distance, right?"

"Right." He laughed.

"By the way, you did a great job changing that tire in record time this morning. You're a handy guy to have around."

"Yeah?"

Alex smiled. "Yeah." He put his hand up and they high-fived each other. "When you get back, why don't you phone the apartment house manager where your mom lives? I'm sure they'll find her so you can tell her you arrived safely."

The teen muttered his thanks, then took off.

The minute Alex heard the garage door open and close, he got Jim on the phone at his house in Mammoth. He could hear their toddler making noises in the background.

"Is this a bad time?"

"No. It's our daughter's fussy time. Janice is about to put her in the tub. Don't tell me you're having problems with Jamal already?"

"No, no. The situation is going surprisingly well all things considered. I'm calling about Ranger King."

"That's right. She's your next door neighbor.

So you've met our resident 'ice princess' already. That's what the guys around here call her."

Alex's brows furrowed. That wasn't exactly how he would describe Gilly King. The hug she'd given Jamal was a hundred percent genuine.

Since a ranger needed to be a college graduate and she'd worked as one for a couple of years, that put her age around twenty-four. Her flawless skin was unreal.

"How did she get that reputation?"

"I knew her in Teton Park before I was made chief ranger here. She's the best female ranger around. Does her job like nobody's business, but after hours there's no fraternizing with the guys. She lost her husband a few years back in a car accident."

Alex sobered at the unexpected news. It explained what she'd meant when she'd told Jamal he reminded her of someone she'd once loved. She'd said it with enough emotion to disturb Alex.

"It was our gain when she was transferred here. One of the divorced Teton rangers went mad and stalked her because she wouldn't give him the time of day. Now he's serving time for attempted murder, but that's another story.

"The point is, there isn't an eligible male in

both parks who hasn't tried to date her, but she's not interested. Since you brought her name up, I thought I'd warn you."

"I've already been warned," Alex muttered.

"The rangers will talk."

"Actually I was put off before I could try." Alex had no one but himself to blame for that. Going after her in front of the tourists was pretty unforgivable.

"Jim? She's had a bad experience again."

"What do you mean?"

"How reliable is the construction company doing the repairs on the park facilities?"

"That outfit from Bozeman has been doing the maintenance for a lot longer than I've been here. I had no reason not to give them the contract for this year's repairs. What's going on?"

In a few minutes Alex had related everything he'd overheard Gilly tell Jamal. "She sounded genuinely relieved we'd moved in to give her some protection."

"Thanks for getting right on this, Alex. I'll call the foreman tonight and investigate it myself. There's only one problem with Gilly. She's too damned attractive. My wife complains that's a sexist remark, but it takes a man to understand."

Alex's teeth snapped. "You got that right."

"I'll get back to you on this."

"Thanks."

"Thank *you*. I'd hate to see us lose Ranger King. She's very knowledgeable and a huge hit with the tourists. That's why I placed her at West Thumb for the summer. So many people begin their park experience there, I like us to put on the best face we can."

Jim knew what he was doing. She had a gorgeous face all right. In fact there wasn't anything about her physical appearance that wasn't absolutely perfect. Jamal had picked her out at once.

The uniform added a touch-me-not element that made a man think…a lot of things he shouldn't.

Worse, he'd already made a false judgment. For that crime he had a feeling he was going to pay. Alex didn't like being in that position.

"Talk to you soon, Jim."

After hanging up, he did the dishes to keep busy, but the activity didn't calm his restlessness. If she'd only been a widow for a couple of years, then the ice princess label probably meant she wasn't over her husband's death yet. The troubling thought didn't help his state of mind any.

He finally went into the tiny third bedroom he'd turned into a study and did some work on the computer. But the second he heard his cell phone ring, he was so wired his body jerked at the sound.

After checking the caller ID, his heart did a swift kick. For her to phone probably meant she was in trouble. He had an idea what kind and picked up on the second ring.

"Ranger King? Is that construction worker still harassing you?"

"Oh, no— That's not why I'm calling. I'm afraid this is about Jamal."

Alex had forgotten all about him. Some guardian *he* made—the old doubts kicking in. He checked his watch. The teen had been gone an hour and a half. Already the boy had broken his promise to be home on time. But maybe he was hurt. At this point Alex's imagination was running rampant.

"What's happened?"

"Well, as I was coming back from Flagg Ranch, I noticed a couple of police cars parked at the side of the highway with their lights flashing. As I drew closer I saw your truck. Jamal was at the wheel."

"Then he wasn't in an accident?"

"No, thank heaven."

Alex let out the breath he'd been holding. That was all the boy's mother would need to hear. His eyes closed tightly. "Where is he now?"

"About five miles beyond the South Entrance to the park. I got out and told the officers I knew Jamal. When I asked what was wrong, they said they'd caught him speeding, and they suspected he'd stolen the vehicle.

"Since they'd barely pulled him over, I told them not to bother trying to find out who it belonged to. After I explained Jamal's situation— that he was only doing a little exploring with your permission—they agreed to let him off the hook this time.

"I got them to promise to keep the incident hushed up. But they won't let him drive the truck home. So, I'm going to bring him with me, and then I'll drive you back to pick up your truck. We're leaving now and should be there in a half hour.

"I just wanted to be sure you were home and knew what was happening before someone else phoned and alarmed you unnecessarily. You know how park gossip goes. If someone passed who hasn't met Jamal, they might jump to an erroneous conclusion."

His hand gripped the phone tighter. "You mean the way I jumped down your throat without knowing all the facts?" he muttered somewhat fiercely. "I'm sorry about that."

"It's all right. Knowing the situation with Jamal helps me understand why you reacted the way you did."

"Then you're a much more generous person than I could ever be." He rubbed the back of his neck absently. She'd just saved him and Jamal a hell of a lot of embarrassment. "I'm indebted to you, Gilly. Thank you," his voice grated.

It wasn't until he'd hung up that he remembered he'd used her first name without thinking.

CHAPTER THREE

GILLY had told Jamal to go sit in her Toyota while she phoned Alex. The man could be a forbidding adversary, but that was a heartfelt apology she'd heard coming over the phone line just now. When he'd said her name, she'd felt it resonate to every atom of her body.

After clicking off, she walked over to the car and climbed in behind the wheel. Jamal darted her an anxious glance.

"Is he going to send me back to Indianapolis?"

Gilly started the engine and pulled onto the highway, waving at the police officers. "Why would he do that?"

He bowed his head. "*You* know why. He told me not to mess with him."

"So why did you? If you want to go home, all you have to do is tell him."

She had to wait a long time for an answer she wasn't expecting.

"I know, but it'll make him mad."

"Why do you care?"

A deep sigh escaped. "He said some guy once helped him out, so he decided to do me the same favor."

"Then if I were you, I'd start showing him how grateful you are for an opportunity I doubt any other teenager in the country has been given. Do it while you can, Jamal. You never know what the future holds."

"What do you mean?"

"I thought my husband would grow old with me, but he got killed two years ago."

His head swerved around. "You were married?"

"Yes. Right out of high school. I was only a year older than you. Kenny and I were together four years. He worked to put me through college." *We lost our precious baby.*

"That period of my life is over and can't be recaptured. Don't let this chapter of your life come to an end before it even starts, Jamal. You could live to regret it."

Silence reigned the rest of the way back to Grant Village. She had no idea if anything she'd said had gotten through to him. Alex was standing outside with another ranger when she turned in his driveway.

"Oh man—" Jamal sounded upset. "I guess everybody knows what I did now."

Gilly's spirits sank, too. The grapevine worked fast. Both men walked over to Jamal's side of the Toyota. It was Larry Smith. He tipped his hat to her.

"Hi, Jamal. Glad to see you're back in one piece."

The teen nodded.

"Someone on the highway saw you with the police and called me. I thought I'd walk over here and keep Alex company till you got back with Ranger King."

"Sorry, Alex." Jamal muttered without looking at him.

"All's well that ends well," she heard Alex say before he added, "This time anyway."

His comment drew Gilly's gaze. She could tell he wasn't sure whether the teen really was sorry, or whether he was just mad he'd been caught. Probably the latter.

Larry extended his hand to Jamal who reluctantly shook it. "You want to come out on night patrol with me next week? Sometimes nothing happens, other times it can get real exciting."

Shock registered on Jamal's expressive features. "Sure."

"Great. I'll be in touch. Good night." He nodded to everyone, then took off for his own house around the corner.

Gilly's gaze switched to Alex who came around to her side of the car. Each step that brought him closer seemed to change the rhythm of her heart. "How about I drive to give you a break?"

At this point she was so affected by his nearness, she decided that might be a good idea. "I think I'll take you up on your offer." In the next breath she'd climbed in back via the gearshift where she could keep her distance from Alex.

He adjusted the seat to accommodate his tall, fit physique before taking her place at the wheel. Then he turned to Jamal.

"I know how attached you are to your baseball cap, but next time you take my car or truck out alone, leave it home."

A look of relief broke out on Jamal's face. "Okay."

"Tomorrow we'll buy you a cell phone so you can call me no matter the hour."

"That would be cool."

Alex studied the teen for a moment. "So…how were the sights tonight?"

"Pretty good."

"Just pretty good?"

"Not as good as last night."

"Get in line for that sight, Jamal. I'm afraid it runs from the far end of Teton Park to the far end of Yellowstone."

"Yeah?"

The two men smiled at each other. Obviously theirs was a private joke. Gilly didn't have a clue what they were talking about. For the thirty-minute drive back to Alex's truck, she listened while he told Jamal about the wildlife he should be watching for en route. He kept both her and Jamal entranced.

When they reached the truck, Alex made a U-turn and pulled behind it. The men started to climb out. Jamal eyed her over the headrest. "Thanks for helping me, Gilly."

"That's what friends are for. See you tomorrow after work."

"I'm your man."

After he shut the door and walked to the truck, she moved to the front of the Toyota and adjusted the seat to fit her five-foot-five frame.

Alex stood next to her open window. She purposely avoided meeting his gaze. She couldn't take the way it made her heart feel, a mixture of excitement and guilt rolled into one.

"Like I told you earlier," Alex said in a low voice, "I'm in your debt for what you did for

Jamal. I'm afraid I'm not cut out for father-hood. Tonight's a case in point."

His unexpected comment brought her head around to face the full force of his intelligent gray eyes. She glimpsed a brief flash of pain in their depths before it disappeared.

"Why would you say that?" she queried softly.

His jaw tautened. "Look what just happened. I must have been out of my mind to hand him the keys and tell to go have a good time for an hour."

"I think you did exactly the right thing," she defended. "He knew the rules and chose to break them, but he realizes you're generous and fair. By getting caught tonight, he's found out exactly what kind of man he's going to become if he doesn't learn lessons from someone like you. These are early days, Ranger La-timer."

"Call me Alex."

She nodded.

"Good night, Gilly," he said in a husky voice before joining Jamal.

Even though they weren't in the same car going home, she felt an emotional connection to him as powerful as her physical attraction. Slowly he was invading her senses, gaining ground toward that special place inside her where she'd thought only Kenny could reside.

She'd made a promise there'd never be anyone else, but somehow Alex Latimer had started to slip past her defenses and was making his presence known.

By the time she'd driven inside her garage, her face glistened with tears. She rested her head against the steering wheel, confused and bewildered by what was happening to her.

Eventually she pulled herself together and went in the house, aware her thoughts were full of Alex, a man who was very much alive. She would be seeing him coming and going. The very thought shouldn't have thrilled her so much.

The next day after work, she'd just set the last batch of doughnuts on the rack to cool when she heard a knock on her front door. She wiped her hands on a dish towel and walked to the foyer. Through the peephole she saw the teen in his signature baseball cap. She'd been expecting him for the last half hour, and opened the door.

"Hi, Jamal. Come on in."

"Thanks."

"You're just in time."

"Smells good."

"As soon as I put on the topping, they'll be ready." She poured the glaze over each doughnut while he watched. "You like doughnuts?"

"Who doesn't!"

She smiled. "My brother Trevor can eat six of these without stopping. Let's see if you can beat his record."

"For real?" he asked incredulously.

"Who else is going to help me?" She put the first batch on a plate and set it on the kitchen table. "Sit down and enjoy yourself. I don't drink coffee, so I don't have any I'm afraid. Would you like milk, juice or water?"

"Milk."

"That's my choice, too."

She poured each of them a glass and sat down to eat with him. "Here's a napkin." The doughnuts started disappearing fast. "So tell me what you did today while you were taking orders from Smoky the Bear."

Jamal must have thought her reference to Alex was hilarious because he slapped his thigh he laughed so hard. When his amusement subsided he said, "He showed me around some geysers."

"At Norris?"

He nodded.

"What did you think?"

"It's awesome."

"What goes on under the ground *is* awesome. You're very lucky to be working with him."

"He was pretty cool about last night."

"I figured he would be."

In fairness to Alex, she realized he was prepared to protect Jamal at all costs, even if it had meant intimidating her in the beginning to show his disdain for assuming she was biased.

"He told me to call my mom this morning. I thought he was going to tell her what happened, but he didn't."

"That would have made her feel bad."

Jamal nodded.

"How is your mom?"

"We didn't talk long. She told me to mind him."

"Since he's the head honcho around here, that's probably a good idea."

Jamal looked confused. "I thought Chief Archer was in charge."

"He's the head ranger. Ranger Latimer is a scientist who's the head of the Yellowstone Volcano Observatory."

"Volcano—"

"That's right. Dr. Alex Latimer is one of the most noted experts in his field in the country."

Jamal shook his head. "Alex never told me anything like that."

Gilly admired the man's modesty. Undoubtedly he was giving Jamal time to absorb everything.

"Not a lot of people realize that lying underneath Yellowstone Park is one of the largest 'super volcanoes' in the world—640,000 years ago it produced an exceedingly large, catastrophic explosive eruption and a giant caldera. The scientists would tell you the park has been on a regular eruption cycle of 600,000 years… so the next eruption is overdue."

His brows arched. "Wow!"

"That's the reason Alex was brought here from Mount Rainier in Washington a month ago. Didn't he explain why a new boardwalk was built at Norris in order to see Porkchop Geyser and Green Dragon Spring?"

"He said something about it getting hotter there."

"Exactly. Certain parts of the park *are* getting hotter. It's Alex's job to monitor the thermal and seismic activity throughout the park. He's the one who determines how safe everything is." She carried the empty plate and glasses to the sink, then turned to him.

"Have you had a chance to meet a friend of mine named Sydney? She's a ranger at Old Faithful."

"No."

"You two have something in common. She was stationed in Indianapolis as a flight attendant before she got the urge to become a ranger."

"Yeah?"

Gilly nodded. "She's in charge of the teen junior ranger program. They meet in the clubhouse across from the Old Faithful Lodge at ten on Mondays. There are about a dozen high school kids from Jackson and West Yellowstone enrolled in the summer program. Do you think something like that would appeal to you?"

"Is she better looking than you?"

She chuckled. "Sydney looks like a world-class model."

He whistled. "I might be interested."

"If you ask Ranger Latimer, I would imagine he'd let you off work to join them."

"What do the junior rangers do?"

Her eyes narrowed playfully. "Show up and find out."

Jamal grinned. She could tell she'd piqued his curiosity. Sydney was great with teenagers. It was the reason Chief Archer had asked her to head the program.

"Maybe I will."

"Good. How do you like Yellowstone so far?"

"It's cool."

Gilly noticed he always said things were cool, even if he didn't mean it. But she had a hunch he'd been honest just now. He was a cute boy. More and more he reminded her of Kenny. Charming and funny without even trying.

Thanks to the man who'd agreed to let Jamal shadow him, the teen was starting to settle in. For both Alex and Jamal's sakes, nothing could have pleased her more.

"Who's cooking your dinner tonight?"

"Alex is. We have to take turns."

Interesting. "I guess you should go home then. Better not let him know you ate eight doughnuts in one sitting. Is he a good cook?"

"His hamburgers were pretty good."

"Pretend you love his food tonight or we're both in trouble." She walked him to the door.

"Thanks, Gilly."

"You're welcome. Come over anytime."

"Okay!"

She watched him jump off the porch and run next door. If she hadn't known her neighbor was making their dinner, she would have asked Jamal to stay. Gilly could have fixed him something nourishing to eat later on. Maybe another time.

While Jamal was still on her mind, she called headquarters to speak to Roberta.

"Hi, Gilly. What can I do for you?"

"I want to order a ranger's summer uniform including the hat in a men's medium."

"A *man's* uniform?"

"Yes. It's for Jamal Carter."

"Oh…Jamal! I met him yesterday. He's cute, but so quiet."

"I imagine he's feeling pretty overwhelmed. I thought if he had a ranger's outfit, it would make him feel more at home here."

"I'm sure you're right. I'll order it first thing in the morning."

"Thanks a million, Roberta. Tell them to courier it overnight to Jamal in care of Ranger Latimer at his house." She didn't dare take it over herself and let her neighbor think she was interested in him. "I'll pay for everything. It's my welcome gift for Jamal."

"What a nice thing to do, Gilly."

"He's a long way from home. Let's keep this a surprise, all right?"

"Understood."

"One more thing. Will you tell them to enclose a little card with this message?"

"Sure. What is it?"

After she gave it to her, Roberta said, "Don't you want to put your name on it?"

"No. Jamal will understand."

"Okay. Consider it done."

"Thanks again, Roberta."

"Hey, there's a box at your front door."

Alex had noticed it the second he'd turned the corner.

At first he thought Gilly must have dropped off some doughnuts like the kind she'd made Jamal four days ago. The ones Jamal hadn't stopped talking about.

The extras Alex had expected she would either have sent home with him, or would have brought over by herself later that night as an afterthought.

But as he pulled in to the driveway, he could see it was an express mail package. Alex wasn't expecting anything in the mail at his home address. Anything official came through headquarters.

Maybe Jamal's mother had sent something to her son, but he knew she lived on a budget that didn't extend to paying for overnight deliveries. Still, Jamal had given her the address and phone number on the phone the other morning....

"Why don't you get it while I put the truck in the garage."

"Okay." Jamal jumped out. Alex had supplied him with a front door key. By the time he entered the kitchen from the garage, a smiling Jamal had joined him carrying the package. "It's for *me*."

"From your mother?"

"No way."

After the unusually hot, humid day that presaged a storm, Alex needed a gallon of ice water and a shower in that order. But because his curiosity was as great as Jamal's, he stayed planted. "Go ahead and open it."

The teen pulled the tab on the outer carton and reached inside for the contents. Out came a little card that fluttered to the floor. Alex picked it up.

For Smoky the Bear's junior ranger. Wear it with pride.

When he finally glanced at Jamal, the boy had replaced his cap with a new ranger's hat. He held a ranger's uniform against his body. "What do you think?"

The hat gave him a totally different demeanor. It had taken a woman to think of it. "I'd say you look pretty good. Who's been calling me Smoky the Bear?" he asked, knowing damn well who it was.

Jamal burst into laughter even before he read the card. Then he said, "I'll give you a clue. It was the woman whose Wyoming license plate number you asked Larry to look up for you."

Alex flashed him a wry smile. "He told you that?"

"Yes. We were talking about Gilly and it just came out."

"You don't miss much do you, Jamal."

"Not when it has to do with hot-looking women."

Probably not for a lot of other things, too.

He glanced at the teen. His remark reminded him Jamal had probably experienced a lot more intimacy in his seventeen years than had Alex in the whole of his relationships with women.

As for Ranger King, it appeared she was full of surprises. "I'd say this calls for a celebration. After we've both showered, let's wear our uniforms to dinner in the Village."

Maybe his neighbor would be out and about.

"You mean it'll be all right if I put it on?"

"As long as you're shadowing me, no one's going to say a word about what we do."

Jamal headed for the other part of the house. Over his shoulder he said, "I guess it's okay since she told me you're the head honcho."

Did she just.

* * *

"Thanks for calling, Mom. I love you."

"I love you, too, darling."

"Give my love to dad. Tell him I'll be flying home in just a few more days."

"The whole family will be together for the first time since Christmas. It'll be wonderful."

"I agree. See you soon."

Gilly got off the phone and went back to the kitchen sink to clean her brushes. One more outdoor session after work tomorrow and the present for her mother would be finished. Once it had thoroughly dried, she'd mount it in the frame and it would be ready to take on the plane.

She glanced out the window several times. It faced both her tiny backyard and her neighbor's. No one was around. She hadn't seen a sign of Alex since the night they'd driven to pick up his truck. It was a good thing, but perversely there was a part of her that kept looking for him coming to and from their houses.

For that matter Jamal hadn't been over since the day she'd invited him for doughnuts. Had Alex discouraged another visit? She hoped not because she was dying to know if Jamal had received his package.

Feeling at a loose end, she happened to look up at the sky and saw clouds gathering.

That didn't surprise her. The air had grown so sultry and close, her T-shirt stuck to her skin in spots.

When she thought of cooking dinner, it held little appeal. Tonight would be a good time to go out for a meal, but she'd have to hurry if she didn't want to get rained on.

After a quick shower, she slipped on her tan pants with the pleats, and a white crocheted top. Normally she wore no perfume because it attracted the bugs. But tonight she made an exception and sprayed on a light floral scent.

Leaving one of the living room lamps on, she headed for the Lake House Restaurant near the shore. Before she reached her destination, sheet lightning lit up the sky, followed by the distant sound of thunder. The storm was moving over the park. It wouldn't be long before it reached this part of the lake.

She parked her car and hurried inside, looking around for her friend Joanna, the assistant manager. Usually she took a break to join Gilly when she came in to eat.

Tonight the place was packed with tourists. There wasn't a seat to be had, and it appeared this was Joanna's night off. The other restaurant in the Village probably had a long waiting line, too. Better to go back home and heat up a TV dinner before she got caught in drenching rain.

"Hey, Gilly—"

She swung around to discover Jamal walking toward her wearing the uniform, and she felt a small swelling of pride that in the hat he could pass for a young, seasonal ranger.

Inordinately pleased she said, "Hey yourself, Jamal."

"I saw you come in. How do I look?"

He was such a poser, Gilly chuckled. "You know you look great."

"Thanks for the outfit. It came to the door a little while ago."

"I'm glad you're happy."

Jamal rubbed his hands together. "How about eating dinner with me?"

"Are you here alone?"

"No. But it's okay. I cleared it with him."

There was only one "him." Her pulse sped up without her volition. "How long have you been here?"

"A long time. Our food still hasn't come."

She could tell this was important to him. "In that case I'd be happy to join you."

They worked their way through the crowded room to a corner table. At her approach, Alex got to his feet. The soft lights from the candles accentuated the strong mold of his appealing masculine features.

How crazy was it that she'd been around park rangers for years, yet the way the trousers of his uniform molded his powerful thighs—the way his standard issue shirt hinted at the well-defined chest beneath—was like a brand-new experience. One that threw her senses into complete chaos, but she refused to let him know it.

Eyeing him directly she said, "Such distinguished company. If I'd known, I would have dressed appropriately."

He treated her to a slow, deliberate appraisal of her face and figure. Not for the first time was she thankful she didn't blush like a young girl. "I have no complaints," came his low, thick response. "Do you, Jamal?"

"No way."

Alex held the extra chair for her to be seated on his right across from the teen. She thanked him in a steady enough voice, but inside she was a trembling mass again, this time from their close proximity and her compelling attraction to him she couldn't deny—even though in her heart she wanted to.

The waitress chose that moment to bring their chicken dinners. "I'll have the same thing," Gilly said when asked about her order.

"Please go ahead and eat without me," she urged them after the woman walked off. "There's nothing worse than cold mashed potatoes and gravy."

"We can stand to wait another minute or two," Alex declared. Jamal immediately took his hand away from his fork. She bit her lip trying not to smile. "Jamal— now that you've impressed Gilly, you can take off the hat until we're through eating."

It disappeared fast. "I forgot."

She kept her eyes trained on the teen. "I'm glad to see the outfit arrived so fast. You know what women say…there's nothing like a man in uniform."

"I didn't know they said that."

"It's a fact, but don't let it go to your head."

He grinned before flicking Alex a glance. "Did you know that?"

Without giving the man a chance to answer Gilly said, "Of course he knew. That's why he became a ranger *after* he became a scientist."

Once again Jamal broke down laughing.

By now the waitress had returned with Gilly's meal which she tucked into with the greatest of pleasure. On cue she noticed their food start to disappear, too.

Suddenly there was a flash of lightning. In

that instant while it lit up the restaurant's interior, her gaze locked with a pair of luminescent gray eyes. Then came the terrific boom directly overhead, knocking out the electricity.

"Whoa—" Jamal sounded spooked. Everyone else around them was reacting nervously, too.

"Don't worry," she assured him. "This happens a lot, especially in summer. Pretty soon the backup generator will kick in and we'll have light again."

"What if it doesn't?"

"Then we'll still stay here and enjoy the rest of our dinner," Alex answered in an unperturbed voice at the same time the rain descended like the heavens had just opened.

There was something so comforting about a self-confident man like Alex sitting there eating as if nothing in the world could shake him, it gave her an unprecedented feeling of safety. If the world were about to end and she could be with only one other person, she'd choose him.

Jamal must have been affected by that quiet strength, too, because she felt his tension vanish. "What will they fix if the generator doesn't work and they can't cook?"

"Sandwiches," Alex supplied.

The waitresses walked around putting up florescent glow sticks to give the room more light.

"I'm sure glad we got here in time. This is cool." Jamal reached for his drink.

She smiled at him. "Another experience to write down in your journal."

He frowned. "Journal—"

"You mean you're not keeping one?"

Jamal looked at Alex. "Am I supposed to?"

Alex stopped chewing. He darted her a penetrating glance before he said, "Not unless you want to, but I have to admit Gilly has hit on an excellent idea."

"I'm not so good at writing."

"Then all the more reason to keep one."

Alex's remark told Gilly where he intended this conversation to go.

"Think how much fun it would be to read your experiences to your family when you get back home. They'll love listening to the many adventures of Junior Ranger Carter."

She noticed Alex's lips twitch.

"Maybe my mom."

Since Jamal hadn't talked about his father, she assumed he had a reason so she decided it was wise not to bring him up.

"There's no maybe about it. Moms adore their children and are naturally curious about everything they do. I never did ask. Do you have brothers and sisters?"

"One sister."

"What's her name?"

"Sharene."

"That's pretty. How old is she?"

"Fourteen."

"I bet she misses you."

"I don't think so."

"Sure she does, but younger sisters sometimes hide their feelings. Do you have pictures of your family?"

"No."

"Well, you'll have to send them a picture of you in your uniform."

That suggestion made Jamal smile. "I'll send one of Alex, too. Will you come over after work tomorrow and take a picture of both of us in our uniforms?"

"Sure," she said, avoiding looking at Alex. "But I'm afraid it will have to be around seven. Do you have a camera?"

"I do," Alex murmured.

Good. She didn't want Alex to think she'd brought up the subject in order to get a snap of him. In truth she'd probably end up ordering a duplicate print.

And then what? Put it next to Kenny's picture? Guilt instinctively pulled her back.

Needing to do something physical, Gilly reached in her purse to pull a twenty and a five from her wallet. Now that the rain had abated and the storm had passed on, it was time to go. She'd finished her meal.

Without hesitation she stood up and put the money on the table. "Thanks for making me a place so I didn't have to stand in line for an hour. Feel free to order dessert. It's on me." She focused on Jamal. "In my opinion the chocolate mousse cake is even better than my doughnuts."

As she turned away, she glimpsed an enigmatic expression coming from Alex's eyes. The fact that he didn't try to stop her filled her with disappointment. If he'd asked to her to stay, she would have stayed seated because she couldn't help herself.

CHAPTER FOUR

"HERE!" Alex tossed a pen and a notebook with a cloth cover on top of Jamal's bed.

The teen had just gotten into his pajamas. His head jerked around. "What's that?"

"A notebook like the kind I use on the job. In your case it's your new journal."

"Oh man— Oops—" He put a hand to his mouth. "I forgot."

"Don't sweat it, Jamal."

He scratched his head. "I don't know what to write."

"The first thing is to note the date and place."

Jamal sank down at the side of the bed and opened it to the first page. He jotted something down, then lifted his head. "Now what?"

"We were at the geyser basin all day. What was your impression of it?"

"It smelled worse than the back of the apartment on garbage day."

Alex chuckled. "That's the H_2S."

"The *what?*"

"Sulphur." He spelled it for him. "It's strong stuff. That's why you saw dead fish. We've had to close up that portion of the lake to the public."

"For how long?"

"Maybe permanently. The animals have been forced to migrate to other regions."

"Can't you do anything about it?"

"Nope. Mother Nature's in charge, just like tonight when the lights went out."

"Oh, yeah. What was the name of that dessert again?"

"Chocolate mousse cake."

Jamal let out a mirth-filled laugh. "How come it's called that when it doesn't look like one?"

Alex felt an emotional tug. Despite Jamal's street smarts, he possessed an endearing naiveté about other things. "This isn't the four-legged kind." He spelled mousse for him. "It's what you call that melt-in-your-mouth chocolate filling."

"It was good, but I like Gilly's doughnuts better."

"Then put that in your journal."

"I'm going to."

Alex decided to leave him to it. "Good night, Jamal."

The teen barely noticed his departure from the room.

Give Jamal a uniform and a notebook, and already he was being transformed before Alex's eyes. All because of a certain female ranger.

Alex would never have thought of either thing. It took a woman's perspective.

But not just any woman's...

A grimace stole over his features. Certainly not Alex's biological mother.

No. This had the unique signature of someone extraordinary. Her name was Gilly King.

Moms adore their children and are naturally curious about everything they do.

In his gut Alex knew she'd be that kind of a mother.

Was Gilly her full name? If so, it was as delightful and different as she was.

By the time Alex was ready for bed, he'd figured out a plan to thank her without Jamal being around. A couple of the rangers had volunteered to take the teen on patrol with them for a few hours.

Tomorrow would be the perfect time for

them to pick him up at Norris. He would make the arrangements first thing in the morning. That would leave Alex free to pursue her. Though he didn't have the need to conquer every woman he met, he wasn't used to being ignored by one who'd gotten beneath his skin.

No woman had ever intrigued him to such an extent before. There were times when she looked at him, he could swear she was interested in him. But her actions said something else. It was difficult to gauge if she held back because she was still too in love with her husband's memory.

Challenged by the mixed signals she sent out, he would track her down and get an answer. From all accounts there was no other man in her life. Yet just the thought of her with some guy who wouldn't be able to keep his hands off her made Alex's sleep fitful. He awakened in a foul mood.

Jamal must have noticed because he gave him wide berth throughout the day. When the rangers showed up at three, the teen acted happy to take off with them. They had an agreement he would be back at the house by seven in the evening.

As soon as Jamal disappeared with them, Alex climbed in his truck and headed for the

West Thumb Information Center. When he arrived and saw that Gilly was finishing up her lecture, he let out the breath he was holding and parked at a distance so she wouldn't notice him.

Within ten minutes the crowd dispersed, except for one male tourist who engaged her in private conversation. Alex knew exactly what the guy was up to.

Once upon a time Alex wasn't averse to getting into a physical brawl if provoked hard enough. For two cents he'd make mincemeat of the guy, but over the years he was supposed to have gained a modicum of civility. He thought he had, but obviously it was a thinly disguised veneer.

Gritting his teeth, he waited until she got rid of the guy and walked to her truck. Soon she was headed in the direction of their houses.

Alex followed at a discreet distance. Though he could be accused of stalking her and he didn't want to scare her, especially because of her past, he'd be damned if he was going to let guilt frustrate his agenda.

At first he thought she was going to stay inside her house. After a couple of minutes he was ready to park in her driveway and ring her doorbell. Then her garage door suddenly opened.

She backed out the truck and roared away. In a few minutes she took a paved road near the West Thumb station that led to a thermal area near the lake where tourists weren't allowed.

He waited until she'd rounded a curve before he continued forward. Images of her flying to meet a secret lover in some romantic tryst away from everyone else got his adrenaline surging.

When he negotiated the curve and came around the other side, he could see no sign of her. What in the devil?

Alex slowed down and reached for the binoculars he always kept in the truck. After scanning the terrain, he spotted Gilly's truck over by a meadow about a quarter of a mile off. She'd taken a dirt road to reach it.

He could leave the truck here and walk the distance. But that might frighten her if he approached on foot. Better to drive and let the sound alert her someone was coming.

Gilly straddled the big log and propped her small canvas in front of her. From the side table borrowed from her barbecue set, she reached for her throwaway palette. When the paint buildup became too heavy, she could toss it and make another one.

It consisted of two foam boards hinged with duct tape. She opened the tubes she wanted and squeezed out tiny dollops of paint. Now she was ready to apply the finishing touches to her canvas.

The air was somewhat cooler today. After last night's baptism, the earth looked cleansed and the individual petals were shiny. Conditions were prime for this last session.

She had to admit that since the advent of Alex Latimer she felt different, as if she'd awakened from a deep slumber. Her senses seemed to have sharpened. Where before she would have admired a colorful meadow, now her gaze thrilled to the sight of so many lavender wildflowers. Each one stood like a little person in the late-afternoon sun.

She had one more flower to fill in. With her brush she carefully applied the paint freehand. The western fringed gentian was Yellowstone's flower. The blue-violet type that grew near the hot springs had no pleats between the corolla lobes and was called the "thermalis."

Since she was stationed in this part of the park, this express flower was special to her.

Gilly was no great artist, but she knew when her mother learned of the story behind the small painting, she would treasure it.

Changing to another brush, she dipped into the Hooker's green, the exact color of the forest floor vegetation. While she was applying it, she heard the sound of a motor coming closer.

This was a no public access road.

Jim had already informed her the construction worker who'd been bothering her was no longer on the payroll. If he stepped inside the park, he'd be arrested on sight.

Relieved by the news, she realized it was probably some rangers out on patrol. She kept painting, hoping they'd leave her alone.

No such luck.

She heard a door open and close, then footfall. When she craned her neck to see over her shoulder, her breath froze in her lungs. There was Alex looking spectacular as usual in a pale blue T-shirt and Levi's jeans.

He'd come alone.

Her heart thumped out of control. "Hi! What brings you out here? Is someone looking for me?"

His handsome dark blond head nodded. "*I* am."

She swallowed hard. "How did you know where to find me?"

"I followed you from the house," he answered bluntly.

"Why didn't you phone me?"

He studied her for a long moment. "Because I wanted to talk to you in person."

"Then it must be serious."

"It is." He put a booted foot on the log, placing a bronzed hand on his knee.

A tremor shook her body. "Has something happened to Jamal? Is he in trouble again?" She hadn't been able to disguise the concern in her voice.

"On the contrary. For the moment he seems to be on the straight and narrow. Because of you he feels so accepted, he's already a different person."

That's what Alex came out here to tell her? She didn't know what was going on with him. It was all she could do to keep her own feelings and hormones under some kind of control.

"Jamal's funny and charming all at the same time. He reminds me so much o—"

"Of your deceased husband?" Alex finished for her.

Her eyes flew to his in surprise. "Did Jamal tell you about Kenny?"

"And Jim. I'm sorry for your loss, Gilly. I've never been married so I can't imagine the pain."

She averted her eyes. Little did Alex know *he* was the source of new pain for her now. One that was filling her with too many conflicting emotions.

"I told Jamal about my husband because we were talking about you. I reminded him that a person never knows what's going to happen in life, so he should take advantage of this unique opportunity to work with the brilliant Dr. Latimer while he could."

"I'm hardly that, but your talk seems to have done some good," Alex murmured. "How much do you know about Jamal?"

"Not much. When he was fixing your truck tire, he told me he was living with you part of the summer."

"Then you need to know all the facts. Jamal's father's in prison."

"Oh no—"

Alex grimaced. "His mother's on welfare. Jamal was truant so often, he was put in an alternative school. Yet on the tests he scored higher than most kids. It made him eligible for a special careers program funded by a private national charity for 'at risk' students.

"I was asked if I would let him shadow me

for a month. This is an experiment for everyone concerned. That's why your help and kindness has been so vital."

"I'm glad you've told me this, but even without knowing, I can tell he's fragile."

"You understand a lot. It must be a female thing. Sending him that uniform was inspirational."

"He looks good in it."

Their eyes met. "I couldn't agree more. Putting it on made him see a whole new list of possibilities he's never considered before. Last night he wrote in his journal until I had to tell him to turn out the light."

She marveled at the revelations. "I thought he didn't have one."

"He's using an extra notebook of mine. I don't know if Jim put us in the house next to you because he knew you'd be good for Jamal. But whatever the reason, I'm glad he did because it's apparent I'm not going to be able to get through this experience alone.

"That's what I came to say, and to apologize once again for putting you on the spot last week during your lecture." He rubbed the back of his neck absently. "I don't nor—"

"Enough said," she broke in. "We've been over this ground already. It's to Jamal's credit he was able to understand what happened and forgive me. So we're all even."

Alex's mouth tautened. "I have another concern. He might start to wear out his welcome with you."

"So that's why he hasn't been over for more doughnuts." She shook her head. "I don't think Jamal would try to take advantage of our friendship. From what I can tell, he's too impressed by you and wants to stay in your good graces."

He eyed her narrowly. "We'll see. I want your promise you'll tell me if you have concerns."

"Of course."

She thought he would leave. Instead he moved closer and hunkered down at her side. His male warmth and the lingering scent of the soap he'd used in the shower teased her senses so much she could hardly breathe.

"Those flowers you've painted look like the real thing. It makes me want to pick one and smell it."

"Thank you." Her pulse throbbed. "I hope that's how my mom feels. I'm making this for her birthday." With another stroke of the brush, she filled in the area beneath the flower, desperate to do something physical because his nearness was making mush of her insides.

Gilly ached for him to touch her. When he

didn't, she reached for the other brush again. "I need to catch the light while it illuminates the purple in the petals. Purple is mom's favorite color. T-this is the reason I told Jamal I'd have to take his picture later."

She was starting to babble.

"Is your family from Wyoming?" he asked quietly.

"No. California."

"Where exactly?"

By now she was feeling shaky. "San Diego area. Del Mar to be precise."

"You're a long way from the surf."

"True. I can't make up my mind which I like better."

"You sound like me. The outdoors is every-thing."

She inhaled sharply. "Where are you from originally?"

"Seattle."

"Puget Sound is gorgeous."

"When were you there?"

If he didn't reach for her in the next few sec-onds, she was going to go into cardiac arrest.

"A few years ago."

"With your husband?"

"With both our families who have seagoing cruisers."

"How long did you know your husband before you married him?"

"Since second grade." Deciding it was impossible to work with him this close to her, she got off on the other side of the log.

Talking about Kenny while her body was crying out to feel Alex's touch was going to destroy her if she didn't end the torment right now.

"I believe this painting is finished! Excuse me while I put it in the truck." For all intents and purposes, it was done. Any touching up she could do back at the house.

Stepping gingerly so she wouldn't crush any flowers, she carried it around the end of the log in order to put distance between them. By the time she'd placed her artwork on the passenger's side of the cab, he'd joined her with the rest of her things.

"Do you want these in the back, or on the floor in front?"

She took the palette from him. "I'll keep this on the floor."

With the kind of masculine grace that was so fascinating to watch, he rested the tray inside the back next to the tailgate. His height made the gesture effortless. She tore her eyes from him, but it was getting harder to be in his company without wanting to be in his arms.

Shocked at the strength of her desire, she hurried around to the driver's side and climbed behind the wheel. "Thanks for helping me," she called out before shutting the door.

Alex drew alongside and leveled a steady gaze on her. "Jamal and I will be cooking hot dogs on the outdoor grill in a little while. You're welcome to join us."

Was he asking her out, or just being neighborly? She wished he would make it clear what he really wanted.

Sucking in her breath she said, "I appreciate the offer, but I have other plans I can't put off. Don't worry. I'll be over in time to take your pictures."

He'd pulled behind her truck. If she traveled in the same direction hers was facing, the dirt road would come out on the highway about a mile from here.

Without waiting for a response she revved the engine and took off.

Jamal climbed in the truck and shut the door. "How come we're taking off work early?"

"Because you've done a great job this week and deserve a treat. I thought we'd go fishing."

He rolled his eyes. Alex had lived with him long enough to know that meant he didn't relish the idea. "I've never been," Jamal said.

"You'll love it. As soon as we get to the house, we'll pack some sandwiches and then head out. I know a spot in one of the fingers of Yellowstone Lake where the cutthroat trout bite so fast and furiously, they practically jump in the boat without being hooked."

He shook his head. "You're making that up."

After they'd driven away from Norris, Alex looked over at him. "Would I lie to you?"

The boy didn't say anything. The thought of fishing with his mentor on a late Friday afternoon didn't appear to have gone down well. Now was the time for Alex to reveal the second part of his plan. "We'll see if Gilly wants to join us."

She'd disappeared the other day after taking two minutes to snap their pictures with his camera.

Even if she'd loved her husband for so many years, Alex could swear she had feelings for him. The sensual tension between them the other day by the lake had been so thick, he had an idea that if he'd touched her, they'd have both gone up in flames. Before this weekend was over, he would find out the truth of her feelings.

"I wouldn't try it."

Advice from a teenager? "Why not?"

"You heard her the first time. No rangers allowed. Bruce says she's got rules."

Bruce was one of Alex's assistants at Norris. Undoubtedly Gilly's name surfaced more often than not during conversations among the single rangers. At this point everyone knew Alex and Jamal lived next door to her.

"Some rules were made to be broken," he muttered. Alex intended to break as many as it took to get her to respond to him.

Jamal slanted him a wry glance. "That's funny coming from you. You want me to find out if she likes you?"

"Thanks for the offer, but I'd better do this myself."

"So far your way's not working," he added cheekily.

Remembering how she'd taken off the minute he'd started asking her questions about her husband, Alex let out a frustrated sigh. "You're right."

"Make her jealous and see what she does."

His head swerved in Jamal's direction. "That works for you?"

"Sometimes."

Alex pondered the teen's suggestion all the way to West Thumb. "If she turns me down today, I'll take your advice and see what happens."

He parked near the Information Center. After writing a brief message on a piece of paper from the notepad in his pocket he said, "Wait for me."

Gilly was still out doing her lecture tour. Ranger Bailey was manning the center where a new crowd had gathered. Alex walked over to him. They both nodded.

"Would you do me a favor and ask Ranger King to call this number the minute her next tour ends?"

"I would, but she's been in San Diego part of this week. I don't know when she's coming back, but she won't be on duty until Monday. If it's an emergency, call headquarters. They should have a number on file where she can be reached."

He crushed the note in his palm. "Thanks for the info."

With teeth clenched, Alex went back outside and got in the truck. They hauled out of there.

When he pulled in the driveway of the house Jamal said, "You don't look so good."

Alex felt like he'd been run over by an eighteen- wheeler rig.

"Didn't she want to go fishing?"

"I have no idea. She's in California."

"What's she doing there?"

"That's where her family lives. She mentioned her mother's birthday was coming up."

"I guess that's where she and her husband used to live, too, huh."

Jamal could always be counted on to speak his mind. But this was one time when Alex could have done without hearing his own thoughts expressed. If she'd known Kenny's family since grade school and they'd all gone on trips together, then she had to be tight with them. Hell.

"What do you say we bag fishing and take in a movie at West Yellowstone instead? We'll grab a hamburger first."

"Sure."

Gilly put her overnight bag in the back of Sydney's Jeep, then climbed in. It was a beautiful evening. The sun had barely gone down below the horizon. "Thanks for picking me up, Syd."

Her friend smiled as they drove away from the West Yellowstone airport. "You did it for me last time I flew to Bismarck. Tit for tat. How was your trip?"

"It's always good to see the family."

"But—"

"I'm glad to be back."

"I bet your mom loved the painting."

"She did. Our family had a wonderful couple of days together. But there was a bad moment at the mall when I ran into Kenny's mother. She didn't know I was in Del Mar."

"I thought you always spent some time with her."

"I always have until this time. She was so upset to think I hadn't called or gone over there, it about killed me."

"Sounds like you've let Kenny go and moved on. His mother ought to know it had to happen."

Gilly bit her lip. "I'm not sure what it means. All I know is, I was happy to get on the plane."

"Because of Alex Latimer."

"Yes," she whispered. "He was all I could think about while I was home. After Kenny, I can't believe I feel this way again, especially when Alex hasn't even—"

"Tried to kiss you?" Sydney finished the sentence. Gilly nodded. "He's probably being careful because of Kenny."

"I'm so confused. It's so hard to tell what to think."

"Since he's your neighbor, you'll find out soon enough. Frankly I'm glad you're back. How about stopping at the Lariat Club for a drink before we go home?"

"The Lariat?" That was a cowboy bar, not exactly their scene.

"Why not? I thought it might be fun to do something totally different for a change. Maybe we'll get picked up."

Sydney was only teasing. Gilly knew that. She darted her friend a concerned glance. "Did you and Chip quarrel?"

"No. It's just that he's been pressing for an answer, and I can't seem to give him one. Maybe I'm over Jarod, but I'm in the habit of thinking I'm not. I guess I want love to grab me by the throat like it did when I met Jarod. Do you think that sounds crazy?"

"I'm the wrong person to ask, Syd. Whatever it is I feel for Alex, it has grabbed me by the throat and won't let go. That's why I didn't want to see Kenny's family—I feel so guilty."

"It's hard seeing Chip's family, too. I know they want us to get married, and I do love him. He's wonderful." She let out a groan. "Isn't it ridiculous to let memories of a forbidden love ruin my whole life?"

Gilly's heart ached for Sydney. She'd fallen for a man she couldn't marry. He was an ordained priest! Her friend was in a terrible place emotionally.

Though Gilly never went to a bar if she could possibly help it, she decided to make an exception in this case because, like Sydney, Gilly

was going through a crisis of her own since
Alex Latimer had come on the scene.

"I'm willing to stop there for a little while."

Her friend shot her a surprised glance.
"You're kidding—"

"Why not."

"Am I ever glad you're home!"

They found a parking spot at the end of the
block, then walked to the other end where they
could hear music outside the club doors. Gilly
had to concede the Lariat's live country and
western band sounded so good, it was no wonder it drew the tourists like mad.

Once inside the packed room, they looked
around only to discover that every table was
taken. By tacit agreement they worked their
way through the crowd to the bar and ordered
their sodas.

While Gilly sipped hers, she watched the
couples on the dance floor. Some were putting
on a show, others slow-danced in place. Some
had on sneakers or sandals, but the majority
wore cowboy boots. Not that they were real
cowboys. Most tourists bought cowboy boots
when they shopped in West Yellowstone just
because they were on vacation and it was fun.

Whether young or old, they all appeared to
be having a great time, especially one young

couple who were really into each other. They were probably still in high school and had used phony ID to get into the club.

Gilly supposed she and Kenny had looked that starry-eyed when they were together. Realizing she'd come a long way out of yesterday, she could hardly relate to that period of her life now.

Feeling as she did, if Alex were to walk in here, she'd probably fly over to him and ask him to dance. Anything to get in his arms.

While her senses reeled at the mere thought of seeing him again, she felt a man's hand clamp on to her shoulder from behind. She smelled alcohol before she heard him say, "You look even better out of uniform if that's possible."

She twisted away, but the action accidentally knocked both her cola and Sydney's out of their hands. Her friend let out a surprised cry as their glasses crashed to the floor.

When Gilly looked up and saw it was the construction worker who'd bothered her before, she was furious. "Drunk or sober, you're a menace. Come on, Syd."

They started for the entrance, once more forced to dodge patrons who hadn't been bothered by the disturbance and were enjoying themselves.

"We're not in the park now," he muttered from behind, grabbing for her waist. In a reflex action she elbowed him in the abdomen. He let out a little grunt, a very satisfying sound to her ears, but he kept on coming.

Then in a twinkling everything changed. The man was suddenly caught in a headlock, and one of his arms was twisted behind his back. She raised dazed eyes to the person who'd subdued him, thinking it was the bouncer.

Her gaze was almost blinded by a flash of molten silver. "Alex—"

He gave Gilly a near imperceptible nod before telling the bartender to call 911.

"Butt out of this—" muttered the man who was squirming without a prayer of getting loose from Alex's steel arm.

"You're under arrest for harassing and assaulting a federal park ranger. The police will take your statement outside. Let's go."

The construction worker looked strong as a bull, but Alex handled him with the precision of a jujitsu expert. He wasn't even breathing hard. By now the crowd had made room for them.

The guy cursed Alex all the way outside the doors. Oblivious, Alex pulled another masterful move, forcing the man to the ground facedown.

Her eyes met Alex's in astonishment. He was impressive in more ways than one. Gilly had to admit she was in awe and felt completely protected.

CHAPTER FIVE

"I THOUGHT Alex Latimer was just a famous volcano expert. I can tell you right now he'd didn't learn those moves through the NPS," Sydney whispered next to her.

Gilly agreed, but the police had arrived, preventing her from discussing it further with her friend. For the next few minutes the sheriff asked her questions and took a statement from Sydney before escorting the inebriated man into his police van.

As it drove off, Alex approached them. "Are you two all right?" Though he'd asked the question of both of them, his gaze zeroed in on Gilly. When he stared at her like that, she had to struggle for breath.

"Thanks to you, we're fine," she answered in a shaky voice.

"What are your plans for the rest of the evening?"

"Sydney picked me up at the airport. We're on our way back to the park."

His eyes darkened, sending a frisson through her body that was part nervousness, part excitement. "Under the circumstances I'll follow you to make certain there are no more unpleasant incidents tonight."

"I won't say no to that," Sydney murmured.

"You're at Old Faithful?"

She nodded.

"Once we reach your place, Gilly can ride with me the rest of the way to the Village."

Gilly almost fainted from excitement. "W-where's Jamal?"

Alex's gaze swerved back to her. "At a chick flick across the street with Ranger Carr's son and a couple of other guys. They'll bring him home later. I'd just left the theater when I saw you two go into the Lariat Club, so I decided to say hello."

"Thank heaven you did," Gilly's voice shook.

"Where are you parked?"

"At the opposite end of the block," Sydney volunteered. "It's the tan and black Jeep Wrangler."

His eyes traveled from Sydney to Gilly once more. "I'll find you." Something in Alex's tone caused her pulse rate to triple.

She started down the crowded sidewalk with Sydney. They didn't speak until they'd gotten in the Jeep and had merged with the traffic headed toward the park. The knowledge that Alex was behind them made her heart thud.

"Tonight you got your answer," Sydney read her thoughts. "Talk about the proverbial knight coming to the rescue of the fair damsel—" Her brows lifted. "After what he just did, I still have goose bumps."

"So do I," Gilly admitted. "In fact I'm kind of terrified, Syd."

"Of what?"

"I don't know. The way he makes me feel when I'm around him. The way I feel when I'm not," her voice trailed off.

"You've just described the way I still feel about Jarod. But in my case, he's forbidden fruit. You don't have that kind of a problem with Alex."

"Except that I feel out of control when I'm around him."

"Is that the way Kenny made you feel?"

"No." She shook her head. "Not anything close. Kenny and I grew up together. We were a girl and boy who just naturally gravitated to each other. I don't remember a time when I didn't love him."

"In other words it was easy, like falling off a log."

"When you put it that way, I guess it was."

"Well there's your answer. Don't get me wrong, but you've never had to work at a relationship. Now an unknown quantity like Alex Latimer has come along. From what I can tell there's nothing easy about him. He's a man, not a kid into games."

Gilly looked over at her. "I know. That's what's got me nervous. I can't sleep. I can't eat. My family knew something was wrong during this trip."

Sydney made a strange sound in her throat. "Those are all good signs you've come back to life. I realize you don't know what the future holds, but I have to tell you I'm excited for you, Gilly."

It wasn't long before they reached Old Faithful. Sydney drove to her quarters and turned in the driveway. Alex pulled in beside them and alighted from the truck. After transferring Gilly's suitcase to the back, he approached Sydney who was standing next to Gilly.

"Jamal told me about the junior rangers' meeting tomorrow. What's the schedule?"

"We'll do projects until one. Then we'll break for lunch at the lodge. Afterward we'll continue to work until four before they go home."

"Mind if I join you for lunch? I sense Jamal would like to see what the junior rangers is all about, but he has this idea the kids don't really accept him because of his background. Tonight he thought the only reason Steve asked him to join him and his friends was because of me. What I'd like to do is show up for lunch a little late so I can watch the interaction while he's not aware of it."

"That's a good idea. You're certainly welcome to show up at any time," Sydney offered.

"Thank you. Where exactly will you and your fledglings be seated?"

"At the big table next to the east windows."

"I'll see you there. Good night."

He turned to open the passenger's door of his truck for Gilly to climb in.

"Good night, Syd," she called to her through the open window. "Thanks again for picking me up."

"You're welcome." Her friend stared at both of them from the porch of her cabin before going inside.

Finally they were alone.

"Alex?" she said as he backed out of the driveway and they headed toward Grant Village. "Thank you for handling that construction worker tonight. I don't know what I would have done if you hadn't been there to stop him."

"Someone else would have stepped in."

"But they didn't. *You* were the one who came to my rescue. I'm very grateful."

"I was impressed with that elbow jab you gave him."

"It still didn't stop him," she half moaned. "When I was training to be a ranger, I didn't learn moves like the ones you applied tonight."

"That's understandable. You didn't grow up a wild kid living on the dark streets of Seattle fighting for your turf."

Gilly stared at him in surprise. "Were you in a gang?"

"No. I operated on my own. God willing, no man will ever assault you again."

Not if Alex was around. From the first he'd been aware of the serious threat the construction worker posed. Tonight he'd dealt with him once and for all. Whatever he'd gone through as a teenager had made him into a remarkable man. Gilly realized no one else could compare to him.

Besides his intelligence and sensational looks, he was a compassionate human being, revered by the other rangers in the park. Much as she looked up to her brothers, she couldn't imagine either of them being unselfish enough to let a teenager live with them, shadow them in their work for a month.

It took a very responsible, self-confident man like Alex to welcome a young stranger into his home and develop a good working relationship with him. From what Gilly had seen already, Jamal appeared to be fitting in and enjoying the experience. That was because of Alex.

He'd said he wasn't cut out for fatherhood, but Gilly begged to differ. Any child would be lucky to have him for a parent.

"How was California?" he asked in his deep voice, bringing her back to the present.

"It was wonderful to be with my family again. Who told you I'd gone there?"

"Ranger Bailey. I dropped by the Information Center to see if you would like to go fishing. That's when I heard the news."

He'd actually sought her out? She pressed a hand to her heart as if to stop it from pounding so hard.

"I see."

"So what did you do while you were at the ocean?"

"We had a beach barbecue for mom's birthday. Did a little water-skiing with my brothers."

"Was Kenny's family there, too?"

"No," she declared. "I'll always love them, but they're having a hard time letting me go. I thought it would be better if we didn't see each other this time."

"Then how about joining me for lunch tomorrow?" He'd changed the subject so fast she was startled. "I would offer to pick you up, but I'll be coming from a meeting at the other end of the park."

The sensual tension between them made it difficult to breathe. "I-I'd like that, but depending on the traffic, I might be a little late."

"I'll wait as long as it takes."

While she was still recovering from that comment, they'd reached his house and discovered Jamal had just been dropped off. He walked over to the truck. Much as she liked Jamal, this was one time when she wished she could have had a few more minutes alone with Alex.

"Hi, Jamal!"

"Hey, Gilly—" He opened her door before Alex could.

She jumped down. "You're just the man I wanted to see."

"How come?"

"While I was in Del Mar, I bought you a present."

"Me? It isn't my birthday."

"Then I guess I'll have to wait and give it to you when it is."

"That won't be until next February."

"Hmm. Well, maybe we could work out a deal."

He rubbed his hands together. "What do I have to do?"

"Carry my suitcase in the house? Then I'll give it to you."

"Are you putting me on?" He sounded happy.

"I would never do that."

"Am I going to like it?"

In spite of her disappointment that the evening with Alex had come to an end before she'd wanted it to, she smiled at Jamal's wonderful sense of humor. "Is Old Faithful still faithful?"

So saying, she hurried over to her house. Jamal's laughter followed. Once she'd opened the door, she walked through to turn on a few lights. The two men soon joined her.

"Just set my case down here on the couch."

When Jamal had done her bidding, she unlocked it using her code and reached inside for the gaily wrapped present. As soon as she handed it to him, he tore off the paper.

Inside was a Lakers jersey which he examined from front to back. His eyes were shining when he looked at her. That's how she knew she'd brought home the right thing.

"How'd you get one with Shaq's name?"

"It wasn't easy."

He gave her a hug that warmed her heart. "I've got to go home and try this on."

"How *did* you manage it?" Alex asked in his deep voice after Jamal had taken off.

"My father's a big Lakers fan. He knows a friend who knows a friend."

His veiled gaze played over her features. "Where's my reward?"

Holding her breath she said, "Unfortunately Dad doesn't know anyone involved with the Seattle Sonics."

"That's all right," he murmured with a faint curve to his lips. "I never was big into basketball. For my reward I'd much prefer going on a hike with you after Jamal goes back to Indianapolis."

So would she, but did she dare to say yes?

"That's only a couple of weeks away now," she speculated as she watched him clean up the gift wrap Jamal had left on the couch. It drew her attention to the play of muscles in his upper arms. Such an unquestionably male physique ought to be outlawed.

"The time's going fast. We'll talk about it over lunch tomorrow," he said before disappearing out her front door. While she stood there in a daze, her cell phone rang.

She pulled it from her purse and checked the caller ID, then clicked on. "Mom?"

"Yes, darling. Are you home yet?"

"Just walked in."

"You sound out of breath. Is everything all right? I've been worried about you."

"I'm fine." I'm more than fine. "Mom? Give me a few minutes to get ready for bed, and then I'll call you back."

"Promise?"

"Yes."

Gilly hung up, still trembling with excitement. Not in her wildest dreams would she have imagined the circumstances that had caused her to end up driving home with Alex tonight. She honestly didn't know how she was going to last until she saw him again tomorrow.

A half hour later she was ready to call her mom. That's when her cell phone rang. She checked the caller ID. It was Alex—

"Hello?" she said in a tremulous voice.

"Gilly? Something's come up that has required me to be in meetings all day. Instead of lunch, I'll take you to dinner. Be ready at four. Wear something dressy."

He clicked off without waiting for her response. Maybe he had other phone calls to make.

Gilly hadn't heard about any meeting, but

that wasn't unusual. The chief never met with all the rangers at the same time. Calling individual groups together to dispense information or discuss policy changes was a common practice.

The storm the other night had caused a power failure at one of the lift stations, sending 177,000 gallons of sewage into a septic tank and then into Yellowstone Lake. No doubt Alex had been the first one to record the findings and send out the alarm.

Emergency crews had to be called in to clean up the spill, but a permanent solution to the problem was to install a backup generator. Maybe that area of the lake was going to be closed off to the public until the new generator was in, thus affecting where she led her tours.

Whatever the reason for the meeting, Alex still wanted to be with her. When she thought about it, she'd much rather go out to dinner with him. Now she could wear the simple black dress with the spaghetti straps she'd bought at the mall in Del Mar earlier in the week. She'd purchased a pair of black slingback high heels to match.

At the time it had seemed a foolish way to spend her money. Thank goodness she'd acted on the whim that had propelled her into the shop. Alex had never seen her in anything but casual clothes or her uniform.

The last lecture of the day ended at four. Gilly cut it short twenty minutes to give herself time to get home. She needed time to shower and blow-dry her hair.

At five after four her doorbell rang. Breathless with anticipation, she grabbed her evening bag and rushed through the house to the foyer. When she answered the door, she had to hold on because Alex was standing there in a navy silk shirt and tan Chinos she'd never seen before.

He looked…incredible. She could tell he'd just showered. It was going to be impossible to keep her eyes off him.

"Are you ready?" His voice sounded husky as his eyes traveled over her in a thorough perusal that left her shaken.

"Yes."

"Then let's go."

He helped her out to his Explorer. Soon they were whizzing toward the South Entrance of the park.

"H-how did the meeting go?"

He darted her a penetrating glance. "Right now I can't remember. You look beautiful, Gilly."

She swallowed hard. "Thank you."

"I've been wanting to be with you like this for a long time."

Her heart leaped. She let out a shaky breath. "If that's true, why didn't you ask me out when you came to the place where I was painting?"

"That didn't count. You had other things on your mind. The kind of evening I have in mind requires your full and complete attention."

"Well I have to admit you've got it now," she said with an honesty that shocked even her.

"I'm not so sure," he fired.

"What do you mean?"

"Until you told me Kenny's family needed to let go, I've felt your husband's memory has kept you at a distance. I've been waiting for the moment when you would start to see me clearly. You've driven me to lengths I've never had to go to before."

For Alex to make an admission like that left her with a fluttery sensation in her chest. "This is all new to me, Alex."

"You think I don't know that?" he bit out. "Only one man in your life since second grade?"

"Even to me it sounds impossible."

"It sounds like a fairy tale, but it's the one you lived. I consider it a miracle you've agreed to be in my company for a little dinner and dancing. Since you're such a private person, I thought we'd drive to Jackson where we're less likely to run into anyone we know.

"While I get a little better acquainted with my next door neighbor, you can remain the untouchable woman of mystery to the others. If you have a problem with that, let me know now and I'll turn the car around."

Alex hadn't risen to the heights he'd attained without possessing those rare qualities that put him at the top of his profession. Men like him made up their own rules of engagement, which was why no one ever got in his way.

When he decided to go after something, it was all or nothing. Despite the fact that she would always love Kenny, a thrill of excitement chased down her spine that for the moment Alex was interested in her. Perhaps finally she was ready to let go of the past, but that thought scared her.

If she remembered it was *only for the moment,* she'd be all right. Temporary relationships were how Alex had maintained his bachelor status all these years.

Now that he'd been astonishingly honest with her, she owed him a certain amount of honesty back.

"I wouldn't be with you if it wasn't what I wanted, too," she admitted in a quiet voice.

His head swiveled in her direction. "Are you saying you'd like to get to know me better?"

"Yes."

"What do you want to know first?"

"Because of Jamal, I've already learned some things about you."

A stillness pervaded the interior of the car. "Like what?"

"He said there was a man who took a personal interest in you, and it changed your life. Who was that?"

"A grocer who gave me about twenty more chances than I deserved. I'm afraid it only proves that someone felt someone like me was worth trying to reform."

Certain things about him were starting to make sense. "Jamal said that was why you took him under your wing."

"The governor of the State asked Quinn Derek to do him a favor. I didn't feel I could refuse."

"I can tell you right now any other park ranger would have found an excuse not to say yes, even if it was the governor who was asking." Her admiration for Alex just kept growing. "You're a wonderful surrogate parent, Alex."

He turned to her with a jaundiced eye, doubt clouding his face.

"It's true," she insisted. "Even though he's been placed outside his normal environment, anyone can see how happy he is."

"I've had help, namely from you."

Though she still felt tension coming from him, it wasn't as fierce.

"Thank you, but the kind of reaction I'm talking about doesn't happen by simple osmosis, so don't give me any credit. I just supplied a couple of externals into the equation.

"You're the one who's made Jamal secure enough not to bolt already. The other rangers admire you for what you're doing more than you know."

"Is that a fact."

"Yes."

"So let's hear about Gilly King's parents. I know you have a mother you adore."

She nodded. "And a wonderful father."

"What does he do?"

"He's the chancellor at USC."

"That reeks of academia."

"You can say that again. The whole family's the same way. Mom's an attorney who's a city court judge right now. Trevor has followed in her footsteps. Wade's a doctor."

Alex's mouth curved upward. "What happened to you?" he asked as they pulled into the parking lot of the Elk Inn in Jackson.

"I'm a throwback, but I still haven't found the ancestor I could be related to."

He smiled. "According to Chief Archer, it was the park's lucky day when you reported for work."

Everything he said whipped up her emotions a little more.

"It was my salvation," she confessed without thinking.

Alex eyed her for a long time through shuttered eyes. "What kind of man was your husband?"

She thought she understood what he was asking. "Turn Jamal into a twenty-two-year-old Scandinavian blonde who carries a surfboard around instead of his Walkman, and you'd have a pretty good idea of Kenny's personality.

"He was the funniest, most fun person in the world. Like Jamal, you could hurt him easily because he was so sensitive. But there was a sweetness in him that made him lovable and able to forgive."

She turned her head toward Alex. "Does that answer your question?"

"In ways you can't imagine," his voice grated.

Amazed that he'd been able to elicit something so private from her when she'd never talked about Kenny with another man, she said, "Let's go inside. The Elk Inn has a country and western band to rival the Lariat Club's. Which reminds me. Have you converted Jamal to country and western yet?"

He flashed her an amused smile. "I'm trying, but he seems to be grounded in rap."

She reciprocated with a smile of her own. "I would imagine 'country' is an acquired taste."

"I did manage to get him to listen to an old Chet Atkins CD the other night."

"Did he like it?"

"He thought it was cool."

"Of course."

"But I'm not sure he's about to run out and buy guitar music any day soon." Alex continued to study her features. "What about you?"

"I like all kinds of music."

"So do I. Let's try out the band, shall we?" On that note he levered himself from the car and came around to help her.

Gilly was glad Alex had brought her here where there was a rustic ambience and lots of tourists. Wanting to be alone with him was too great a temptation right now. Each little revelation made him stand out more in her mind and heart. If she wasn't careful, she could be swept away by him.

Once inside, they wound their way through reception and down the hallway to the dining room. After the hostess had seated them, the waitress came right over to the table to take their orders.

The second she walked off, Alex didn't waste any time asking Gilly to dance. She'd been waiting for this moment all during the drive, but the minute he drew her into his arms, she realized it was a huge mistake.

Every line and curve of her body seemed to be molded to his hard-muscled frame. The floor was so packed they were forced to dance in place. She almost fainted when he lowered his smoothly shaven jaw to her flushed cheek.

No matter how close a shave, it was a man's cheek, a man's strong physique melded to her figure, a man's heart pounding against her own, reminding her of the fundamental differences between them.

Like a tsunami ripping across the ocean, wiping out the normal flow of the current in its path, desire coursed through her body erasing all existing barriers by its sheer force.

Having lost all track of time, she followed his lead in a kind of rapturous haze. Sometime later she saw the waitress putting food on their table.

"Our dinner's being served," she stammered, almost giddy from his touch.

"I noticed." Instead of making a move to let her go, his hands roved over her back, gathering her even closer.

"The steaks are going to get cold. Why don't we eat and then dance some more?" She didn't dare remain this close to him any longer.

"Promise?" he whispered against her earlobe. The sensation sent fingers of delight down her neck to infiltrate her bloodstream.

"Yes," she said on a shallow breath.

"I'm going to hold you to it," he vowed.

Her body was sending signals that she was enjoying this way too much. They made it easy for him to read her thoughts which were warning her to break this up before she couldn't!

Alex kept a grip on her hand as he led her through the crowded dance floor to their table.

Maybe it was being with him, but Gilly scarcely noticed what she was eating. He, on the other hand, attacked his steak with apparent relish.

Before long the waitress came by to take their dessert order. No sooner had she walked off again than his cell phone rang.

His gaze locked with hers, anxiety filling his eyes. "I'm off duty, so unless an emergency has arisen, it must be Jamal."

He pulled the phone from his pocket to check the caller ID. Her heart plunged when she saw his face suddenly pale.

"What it is?" she cried, but he'd already clicked on.

Sick with fear, Gilly waited to hear what the phone call was all about. She didn't have to wait long.

"That was the E.R. calling from the hospital here in Jackson. I don't know the whole story, but part of Jamal's foot got scalded in one of the thermal pools."

"No—" Gilly cried out in horror.

He threw down some bills. "Let's go!"

CHAPTER SIX

GILLY jumped up from her chair. Together they ran out of the dining room past surprised diners. Within minutes they'd pulled into the emergency area of St. John's Medical Center.

Gilly hurried inside the doors with him. The second Alex informed the triage nurse who he was, she showed them to the cubicle where they found Jamal surrounded by three other people. His foot had been elevated. She could see he'd already been treated and they'd inserted an IV.

"Thank God, you're alive," she heard Alex whisper.

Jamal held up a weak hand to high-five him. He was obviously relieved that Alex had come, but he looked scared, too. Gilly's heart went out to him.

The man on the other side of the bed rose to his feet. "Dr. Latimer, I'm Ray Lewis. This is my wife, Louise, and my daughter Cindy. Before you jump to any conclusions, I want you to know our family will take full responsibility for this."

The girl named Cindy looked like she'd been sobbing. Her face was all splotchy and her eyes were puffy.

"It was my fault Jamal got hurt. I know better than to step off the trail onto the crust. I was just showing off for him. He got angry and pulled me back to the walkway, but his foot slipped and it broke through the surface." Once more she was convulsed in tears.

"Hey—" Jamal called out. "It was no big deal. Just my foot got wet."

"Jamal saved our daughter's life," Mrs. Lewis said. She held on to Jamal's fingers so she wouldn't disturb the IV. She, too, was eyeing him tearfully.

Gilly felt Alex place his hands on her shoulders from behind. She knew the gesture was unconscious, that he needed support.

"I didn't mean for him to get hurt," Cindy half sobbed.

"Of course you didn't—" Alex replied. "Let's all be grateful nothing worse happened." Gilly felt him struggling for breath. "Since there's been enough excitement for one night, I suggest we let Jamal get the sleep he needs. By morning he'll probably be ready for visitors."

"Come on," Gilly said. "I'll walk you out." She knew Alex wanted time alone with Jamal.

There was no question the three people were devastated, particularly Cindy. "Today was my first day at the junior rangers' meeting," she volunteered in a tremulous voice. "I can't ever show up there again."

So that was how she and Jamal had become acquainted!

Gilly slipped an arm around the girl. "Of course you can. After what happened tonight, I'd say you'll make a better junior ranger than ever. You've seen the dangers firsthand and can speak from experience.

"Don't let this accident burden you. Learn from it. Besides, I know Jamal very well. He would never blame you. It's not in his nature."

The girl eyed her mournfully. "How do you know him?"

"Because he lives next door to my house with Ranger Latimer."

"You're Gilly!" she cried.

"Yes."

"He says you're cool."

Gilly couldn't help but smile. "He's a terrific guy and a real hero."

Cindy nodded. Her eyes filled up again. "I feel so awful. What can I do for him?"

"Bring him some doughnuts. He loves them."

"Okay. I will. Please tell him again how sorry I am?"

"I will."

The girl reached in her jeans and handed Gilly a set of car keys. "These belong to Dr. Latimer. I parked his truck outside the E.R. when I brought Jamal in."

"I'll make sure he gets them." She walked Cindy and her parents to the sliding doors of the main E.R. entrance. Once they were gone, she headed for the desk where one of the doctors was working on a chart.

"How badly was Jamal Carter scalded?" she asked as she put the keys in her purse.

The man looked up. "He's lucky. Because he caught himself in time his toes only suffered second degree burns."

"Considering the circumstances, that's wonderful news."

"I agree. They're not deep, but they're painful. After we put a temporary walking cast on him, we'll release him tomorrow and send him home with crutches and antibiotics. For the first twenty-four hours he'll need to rest his foot. Then he can use crutches to get around.

Bring him back in a week and we'll remove the cast."

"Thank you for the care you're giving him. His mother lives in Indianapolis, so he doesn't have family around."

"Luckily the girl he jerked to safety had the presence of mind to help him make it to the truck so she could drive him here immediately. Her quick thinking made it possible to get the cold water treatment started faster."

"I'll remind Cindy of that when she calms down." Anything to help assuage her guilt. It wasn't every day an accident like this happened.

She left the desk and rushed back to the cubicle. As she let herself inside the curtain she heard Jamal say, "It was hot!"

Gilly's eyes met Alex's in shared horror of what might have happened. Then she leaned over the teen and hugged him hard. "We love you, Jamal. I'm so thankful you're going to be all right."

"Me, too. It scared the begeebers out of me."

"Are you in pain right now?"

"No." His eyes sought Alex's. "Hey Alex? I don't think my mom better hear about this."

"Let's see. Perhaps later on when you feel better, you can write it in your journal. By the time she reads about it, you'll have been recovered for a long time."

"When can I go home?"

Alex gave her another soul-searching gaze before he looked at Jamal. "As soon as the doctor gives you the okay to leave, Gilly and I will fly back to Indianapolis with you."

His inclusion of Gilly sped up her pulse.

"No way— I meant to *our* house."

Alex couldn't be in doubt how Jamal felt about him.

"I just talked with the doctor," Gilly broke in. "He said you'll be released tomorrow provided you get your sleep tonight and there are no complications."

"Good. I hate hospitals."

"We all hate them," Alex murmured, "but tonight it's the only place you should be."

"It's okay if you want to leave now."

"I'm not going anywhere," Alex assured him. "I plan to stay right here with you."

"Are you putting me on?"

"Would I do that?" Alex came back in a husky voice.

"All night?"

"Do you think I could get any sleep tonight knowing you are in here?" he demanded.

"Tell us about Cindy," Gilly prodded in a

gentler tone, sensing that Alex's emotions were close to breaking the surface right now.

"She'll be a senior this fall like me. After the junior rangers' meeting, she called home to see if she could stay longer so we could mess around. Her parents said they'd pick her up at eight in front of the Lake House Restaurant."

"I thought you said the kids didn't like you," Alex teased him.

"Yeah, well I guess I figured wrong where Cindy's concerned."

"I guess you did. From what Ranger Taylor told me earlier today, there were quite a few kids enjoying your company, including Steve. So, what did you and Cindy do for fun before she led you astray?"

"We went on a drive in the truck, and got some food. Later on she said she wanted to go over by the thermal pools. I told her we weren't supposed to go near them without permission.

"She asked me if I always did everything you told me to do, then she ran off. That made me mad so I followed her.

"I told her what you said about that couple who veered off the path last year and slipped through the crust. But Cindy just laughed and told me I was a city boy.

"When she said that, I told her she was crazy

and yanked her back. That's when I…felt like my…toes were on…fire…."

By now Jamal's eyes had closed. The sedative had started to work. He'd stopped talking.

Gilly glanced at Alex standing across the bed from her. She knew what was going through his mind. No ranger would ever forget that particular park accident at one of the hot pools. The woman had died, and the man was hovering close to death right now. It was the stuff nightmares were made of.

Alex looked so drawn, it alarmed her. They'd all received a terrible shock, but he was the one responsible for Jamal. He'd taken that role to heart. Like a father…

"How do parents survive childhood?"

Tears rose in her throat. "After our baby was born dead, I asked the same question, but I'm still here, so I guess parents are made of sterner stuff than we know."

"Gilly—"

In the next breath she found herself in his arms. "I didn't know." He cupped the back of her head while he rocked her for a long moment. "When did it happen?"

"A year after we were married."

He clutched her tighter. "You've suffered."

Gilly agreed, but the man holding her right

now had brought her out of yesterday. She was a different woman today.

Though she wanted this moment to last forever, she was afraid someone would walk in on them. Slowly she eased out of his arms. "It's all in the past, Alex. I'm just so thankful Jamal's injury isn't life threatening."

A grimace marred his handsome features. Beneath his tanned skin he still looked pale. "If anything had happened to him, I don't know how I could have faced his mother."

She shook her head. "Stop thinking about that. He's going to be fine. You're the one I'm worried about. Sit down in the chair before you fall," she ordered quietly.

To her amazement, he actually obeyed her. She watched him rub his forehead. "I could never be a father," he muttered.

His words sounded as if they'd poured from his soul, but Gilly didn't believe for a moment he really meant them. He was in shock and was simply reacting to the near tragedy because Jamal was in his care.

"I'm going to bring you something to drink. I'll be right back." But when she returned with a soda, he'd fallen asleep. He needed rest more than he needed anything else.

She set the drink down on the cart. Her gaze

wandered from Jamal to Alex. After studying the lines and angles of his rugged face for a few more minutes, she left the hospital and drove back to the park in Alex's truck.

In five hours she would have to be on duty. Fortunately Alex still had his car so he'd be able to drive Jamal home when he was released.

Once she reached their street, she pulled in Alex's driveway and parked on the left so he could get his other car in the garage when he arrived. Then she hurried into her house.

After setting her alarm for seven-thirty, she went straight to bed. Yet she knew her mind wouldn't be able to turn off. Too much had happened between her and Alex. And now there was the whole ghastly accident involving Jamal….

No matter how much Alex would hate it, she feared it was only a matter of time until word of it became public knowledge. While she'd been getting him a drink, she'd asked the staff in the E.R. to keep the news quiet. But everyone knew hospitals were notorious dens of gossip. She doubted they would honor her wishes.

That was only one of her troubling thoughts before she fell asleep. After being in his arms earlier, the words he'd said about never wanting to be a father still played in her mind. Surely he hadn't meant them—

At five to eight the next morning, she entered the Information Center office half-dead and bleary eyed. She couldn't believe her first tour would be starting shortly.

Ranger Bailey flicked her a glance, then did a double take. "Are you okay?"

"Sure. Why do you ask?"

He grinned. "You don't usually wear your uniform with the blouse hanging out."

"Oh—thanks for reminding me." In her haste to get here on time she'd forgotten to tuck it in. While she hurriedly fixed herself and applied her lipstick, the phone in the office started to ring.

It had to be eight o'clock. That's when the public invaded and all the rangers were on call until they went off duty.

"Ranger King? It's for you." He handed Gilly the receiver.

"Ranger King speaking."

"Gilly?"

Her body trembled. It was Alex. His voice sounded decibels deeper than normal, causing her legs to almost buckle.

"Why in the hell did you leave?"

Her heart pounded outrageously. Clutching the phone tighter she said, "There wasn't anything more I could do last night. When I left the cubicle, you and Jamal were sound asleep."

"How did you get home?"

"In your truck. Cindy gave me the keys."

"I forgot all about it. You shouldn't have had to drive home alone that late at night—especially after your experience with that construction worker."

She smiled. "I'm a ranger, remember? I can take care of myself."

He muttered something close to unintelligible.

To get him off the subject she said, "Tell me about our patient."

"He's moaning because the doctor hasn't been around to release him yet."

"That's the best news I could have heard."

"Jamal was disappointed when he woke up and discovered you'd gone. You could have asked another ranger to cover for you today."

Alex's mind was distinctly one-tracked this morning. "I would have liked to stay, but I didn't want to lie about the reason why I couldn't report for work. The less talk there is about the accident, the better."

"I have news for you. It's too late. Jamal's heroics have made the morning headlines on the local TV news. By tonight it will be national news"

As Gilly groaned, Ranger Bailey whispered that her group was ready and waiting for her.

"I have to go."

"I know. Come over to the house when you get off duty." The line went dead.

With her adrenaline gushing, she put the receiver back on the hook and dashed outside to begin her tour. It was followed by two more, keeping her so busy she was forced to push thoughts of Alex to the back of her mind.

At noon she returned to the Information Center to eat the sandwich she'd packed for lunch. To her surprise Larry Smith motioned for her to step into the back room. It served as a storage and lunchroom with a minifridge.

She assumed he'd heard about Jamal's accident and wanted to get some details from her to pass on to Chief Archer.

"It's good to see you, Gilly." He closed the door.

"If this is about Jamal, it wasn't his fault," she said without preamble.

Larry smiled. "We all know what happened. When he gets better, the chief's going to honor him for what he did."

Gilly couldn't have been happier to hear that news. "He'll love that. Maybe we can send for his mom and sister to surprise him."

"I don't see why not, but that's not the reason I was waiting for you. The chief has called a meeting with some key people and wants you at headquarters as soon as you can get there. This is important. I've already arranged for another ranger to take over your tours this afternoon."

Under the circumstances, it was a good thing she hadn't asked for the day off.

"Is this about that construction worker Ranger Latimer had arrested in West Yellowstone for harassing me?"

"No, and I'm afraid I'm not at liberty to explain. Since I have one more ranger to visit, I'll take off now and see you at Mammoth."

"Okay."

Gilly took her sandwich from the fridge and followed him out the door. After waving to Ranger Bailey, she left the center and walked to her truck, wondering what this was all about.

Most meetings were posted. For Larry to seek her out personally without telling her the nature of the meeting meant this wasn't only something out of the ordinary, it was classified.

With summer upon them maybe the governor or one of the senators was bringing his family or another prominent dignitary from Washington, D.C., for a visit. It forced all park personnel to step up security and put on their best face.

There was only one problem. Alex would be expecting her to come by after work to see Jamal. Since she might not make it back in time, she decided to call him on his cell phone, but it was turned off and so was his voice mail.

Maybe he was still at the hospital. She remembered they didn't allow people to use them inside the building.

On the chance that he'd already brought Jamal home, she phoned Roberta for Alex's home phone number. When she tried it, he didn't pick up there either. Perhaps he and Jamal were on their way from Jackson and had hit a spot where there was no service.

The only thing to do was wait until she reached Mammoth. Depending on the length of the meeting, she would ask to be excused long enough to talk to Alex and explain why she might have to be late.

At one-thirty she rolled into the parking lot and hurried inside headquarters. Roberta gave her a nod. "In the conference room. They're just starting."

Relieved she wasn't late, she opened the door. Beth waved her over to the rectangular conference table. Sydney was there, too. They'd made a place for her between them.

With one glance Gilly spied the superintendent, Chief Archer, the seasoned rangers from all areas of the park like Bob Carr—and two men she didn't recognize who were dressed like tourists.

As Chief Archer stood up, Larry Smith slipped inside the door and took his place at one end of the table.

"The superintendent asked me to call this meeting. I want to thank all of you for getting here so fast. We're only missing Ranger Latimer who's been excused due to unavoidable circumstances."

He looked around, eyeing each one of them soberly. "What goes on in this room, stays in this room. You know what I'm saying."

A little shudder passed through her body.

"At this point I'll turn this portion of the meeting over to the superintendent."

Gilly had met and talked with Quinn Derek on several occasions. He usually wore a smile, but today his grave countenance could be described as austere.

"Good afternoon to all of you. I've brought two FBI agents with me, Agent Dunn and Agent Montoya. There's a sniper on the loose. He's already killed three people along the highway between Salt Lake City, Utah, and Rexburg, Idaho. Through various phone tips, the

FBI believes he's headed north and will shoot again.

"In case his next destination is the Tetons or Yellowstone, both parks are swarming with undercover agents as I speak. Your job is to stay alert and report anything that looks or seems suspicious.

"These men are going to brief you on the details of what they know so far. If everyone does their job, then our safety can be ensured. Suffice it to say that, as of now, the park is on the highest security alert."

Gilly's thoughts darted to Alex. She imagined he and Jamal were home by now. The selfish part of her was glad the teen had to stay indoors. Alex would be forced to wait on him. Both of them would be safe. In a very short time they'd become precious to her.

Alex carried the tray of food into Jamal's bedroom and set it down across his lap. A cushion from the couch made the perfect prop for his foot.

"Eggs and bacon for dinner?"

"You've never had breakfast at night before?"

He shook his head.

"Shall I eat both our plates then?"

"No way—" He smiled. "I'll try anything once."

"Think you've got room after the doughnuts Cindy brought to the hospital this morning?"

"I ate those hours ago."

"Just checking."

Alex sat down on the chair near the bed and they both tucked into their food.

"I thought you said Gilly was coming over."

"She'll be here as soon as she can."

When she hadn't appeared by quarter after four, Alex made a call to the West Thumb Information Center and discovered she'd left at noon following a visit from Larry.

That news prompted Alex to phone headquarters. Once Roberta told him the VIP meeting had broken up, he asked to speak to Jim. His friend asked for a rundown on Jamal first, then he told Alex the sobering news about the sniper.

After they'd hung up, Alex purposely planted himself on a chair where he could see out of Jamal's bedroom window. It faced the side of Gilly's house. When she pulled the truck in to her driveway, he'd know about it.

What he didn't expect was to hear his front doorbell ring. Had she parked in his driveway? He swallowed the last bite of bacon and strode swiftly through the house to open the door.

Forced to recover from his disappointment that it wasn't Gilly, he greeted Steve Carr and his friend Joe Tobler who lived in Gardiner. They'd driven down from Mammoth to see Jamal. TV or not, word traveled fast through the park grapevine.

Jamal had more friends than he knew. Their appearance would please him almost as much as it pleased Alex.

"We brought him a new CD he might like. Can he have company?"

Alex nodded. "He'll be happy to finally have someone fun to talk to." The boys laughed. "Come in. His bedroom's the first door down the hall on the right."

"Thanks." They rushed past him.

As Alex was about to shut the door he caught sight of Gilly's truck. She'd just rounded the corner of the street. Relieved Jamal would be entertained for a while, he shut the door and walked across his driveway to wait for her.

She couldn't have had more than a few hours sleep last night. Yet when he opened the driver's door for her after she'd pulled in her garage, he knew it wasn't fatigue alone that had robbed her complexion of its natural glow. The garage door closed behind them.

"Hi," she said after she got out. Alex could

tell by her body language how tense she was. "I'm sorry I'm late. Will you tell Jamal that as soon as I've freshened up, I'll be over to see him?"

"He has company right now. Why don't you and I go inside your house where we can talk privately."

The expression on that beautiful face of hers grew anxious. "Has he developed complications after all?"

"He's fine, Gilly. You're the one I'm worried about."

"Why?"

The question belied her next action which was to rush around the end of the truck and hurry inside her house through the connecting door. He followed her into the kitchen, a replica of his own.

"Would you like a glass of water?" She'd already poured herself one from the tap.

"No, thank you."

"I needed that," she sighed after draining it, but she avoided his eyes.

He moved closer. "I know where you've been and why. You don't need to worry. Nothing's going to happen."

His words caused her head to rear. Her haunted blue gaze shot to his. He could tell she was having difficulty holding back her emotions.

"You can't know that for sure."

"It's one man. He's either driving a red or blue truck with Idaho license plates. No matter what, he'll never make it past the first entrance."

Though he hadn't touched her yet, he sensed her fear. Out of a driving need to reassure her, he wrapped his arms around her and crushed her against him.

The sweet scent of her apricot shampoo still clung to her hair which glistened a rich brown in the overhead light. He buried his face in it the way he'd longed to do last evening while they'd been dancing. That seemed a lifetime ago.

"We're on top of it, so there's no reason to worry about anything."

"No reason—" she cried against his shoulder. "I remember a sniper incident on the L.A. freeway a few years ago. It took months before he was found. I couldn't bear it if anything happened to…someone I cared about," she added lamely

She finally lifted her head. Her deep blue eyes seemed to take up her whole face. "Oh boy. I-I'm afraid you've caught me in a moment where I've been overreacting."

"After the losses in your life, I understand where all this emotion is coming from."

"Some ranger I make. I feel like an idiot." But the fear of losing someone else she cared about slammed through her.

"If you think everyone else went home from that meeting without giving it a second thought, then I have news for you. Tell me what Quinn Derek told you. Did he speak at the meeting?"

"At the end."

"He was the one to listen to. What did *he* say?"

She lifted her head. "Not to be alarmed. Just let the police and undercover agents infiltrating the park do their work and everything would be fine. All we had to do was keep our eyes and ears open to anything we found unusual and report it to him or Larry or Jim."

"Exactly. Nothing's going to happen to anyone. If I believed for one moment you were in danger, I'd haul you out of here so fast you wouldn't have time to look for your purse."

She stared at him for a long time before her body relaxed and her lips formed a faint smile he found utterly seductive. "Is that what we female park rangers do?"

"It's what a woman does. Sorry, but in my eyes you're a woman first. If you have a problem with that, I can't help it anymore than I can help wanting to kiss you. It's been a temptation to me ever since I saw you filling up your car at Grandy's."

Recognition of that moment flickered in her eyes before he caught her face between his hands and lowered his mouth to hers.

"Alex—" he heard her cry. Whether in protest or shock or both, he couldn't decipher. All he knew was that this gorgeous woman was finally in the place he wanted her—tangled in his arms where he could hold her curving warmth against him. Nothing was going to prevent him from kissing her long enough to uncover any secrets she was still keeping from him.

When her lips suddenly parted to allow him deeper access, it almost undid him. Beyond caution now, Alex gave in to his long suppressed hunger, molding her to him as they gave each other kiss after kiss, each one more smoldering than the last.

He lost track of the time as they stood in her kitchen while he indulged in this communion of hands, mouths and bodies. Alex had known desire before, but this was more than a physical coming together of a man and woman who found pleasure in the stolen moment.

It was so much more in fact, he couldn't begin to find the words, let alone describe the state of his emotions.

"Don't pull away from me yet," he begged the minute she tried to ease out of his arms. The measure of his entrancement was so great, he couldn't comprehend not continuing this escalation of excitement. He'd never experienced anything like it in his life.

"We can't do this—" she cried on a ragged breath. "We've been over here so long, Jamal's going to wonder what happened to us!"

Jamal—

Alex stifled a groan. He was so far gone he'd forgotten everything, including the teen who was lying on the bed in Alex's house pretending to be tough in order to hide his pain.

Before he was ready to let her go, she moved out of reach. "I'll be over in a few minutes." The next thing he knew, she'd dashed from the kitchen toward the other part of her house.

If it weren't for Jamal, Alex would remain where he was until she reappeared. He ached for the magic to continue. Something had happened just now…

As he reluctantly let himself out the front door of Gilly's house, he realized he could never go back to the person he was a little while ago.

CHAPTER SEVEN

THE Honda Steve Carr had driven was still parked out in front of Alex's house. When he walked inside he could hear rock music coming from Jamal's room. He checked his watch. It was quarter to eight. By the time the boys drove back to Mammoth, it would be getting late.

After a detour to the bathroom where he kept Jamal's painkiller and antibiotics, he joined the threesome who were deep in some discussion.

"Hey, guys." They nodded to him. His gaze flicked to Jamal. "How are you feeling?"

"Good."

He probably was. Having friends drop by was potent medicine, too.

"Has Gilly come home from work yet?"

"Yes. She'll be over soon."

"Cool."

"It's time for your pills." He handed Jamal a glass of water and his medication, wondering when his visitors would leave. But it seemed they weren't in any hurry to go. As long as it was all right with Steve's father, Alex didn't mind.

"What time did you guys tell your parents you'd be home?"

"Ten."

The doorbell rang. Alex's heart thundered with a suffocating force. "I'll get it."

He hurried through the house to the front door. When he flung it open, he discovered Gilly had replaced her uniform with a pair of pleated white pants and a short-sleeved top in a deep plum color. It didn't matter what she wore. On her, everything was stunning.

"Come in."

"Thank you." She closed the door. "Is Jamal still awake?"

She'd had enough time to assume her bright, professional persona, but Alex was very much aware she couldn't meet his eyes. This time he knew why and was reassured by the tiny pulse at her throat. It was visibly throbbing with a life all its own.

"He's got friends entertaining him."

"I wondered whose car was out in front."

"Hey, Gilly—" Jamal called to her from the bedroom.

"Hey, Jamal—" She headed down the hall. Alex strolled behind her, enjoying the view. The boys gave her an enthusiastic greeting as she entered his room.

"Hi guys.

"What?" she exclaimed with exaggerated surprise. "I thought for sure someone would have brought along their games console for me to play."

"Dad took mine away," Steve admitted.

"What's your excuse, Joe?"

"Mom only let's me use it two hours a week."

She stared at Jamal with her hands on her hips. "I guess Smoky the Bear doesn't have one hiding around here anywhere."

Jamal grinned. "No way."

"I thought not. I guess we'll just have to play a couple of rounds of poker."

"Poker?" Steve looked shocked. "I thought rangers didn't do things like that."

"I'm off duty, and I just happen to have a deck of cards in my trusty purse.' She flashed Alex a teasing glance. "Are you in, or out?"

Alex had been lounging against the door-jamb with his arms folded, loving the way she lit up a room and engaged everyone so they felt good.

"Definitely in."

"Okay—" Gilly sat down on one side of the queen-size bed. Alex took the other. "We'll play a couple of hands of Spit in the Ocean to get the hang of it, then we'll get serious."

Steve laughed. "Where did you learn that game?"

"A guy on the beach. In summer he would get people to play for pennies. By the end of the day he'd wiped everyone out."

"Fantastic!" Jamal exclaimed.

"He was indeed, but if you guys tell your parents anything about this, I'll deny it."

They burst into laughter.

She had everyone mesmerized, most of all Alex. Unfortunately he was aware of the passing time. Much as he hated to be the bad guy, after twenty minutes he had to put a stop to their fun. The boys moaned in protest.

Gilly put the cards back in her purse. "If you guys get home on time, we'll be able to do this again."

"Tomorrow?" both teens said in unison.

"That's up to Alex."

He got up from the bed. "Let's see how Jamal is feeling tomorrow and go from there."

"Okay. We'll call you, Jamal. Hope you feel better."

"See ya, Jamal. See ya, Gilly."

Alex walked them to the door. When he returned to the bedroom, Gilly was helping Jamal with his crutches so he could make it on his own to the bathroom.

Once they were alone, she eyed him anxiously. "What are you going to do about Jamal while he's recuperating?"

"I already have a plan if you're willing."

"What is it?"

"If you'll watch out for him during the day, I'll be back by four to relieve you. It'll require freeing up another ranger to take over your tours for the week—but that will be easier than me taking time off."

"I love Jamal. Provided the chief says it's okay, I'd be happy to stay with him."

That's what Alex had been hoping to hear. It would keep her and Jamal out of the sniper's way, and it would keep her here…under his roof. "Good. While you help Jamal back to bed, I'll phone Jim and run the idea by him."

Not waiting for her response, he walked to the kitchen and got Jim on his cell phone. After explaining the situation, Jim told Alex to put Gilly on the line.

Alex went back to the bedroom. "Gilly?"

"Yes?" She'd just arranged the cushion in a comfortable position beneath Jamal's foot.

"The chief wants to talk to you. Go ahead and use my phone."

Their gazes held before she took it from him and wandered into the hall.

Jamal's eyes followed Alex as he arranged the quilt over him, taking care not to let it touch his toes which were being allowed to heal naturally.

"What were you two doing at her house earlier?"

"How did you know about that?"

"The guys saw you go in her garage. You didn't come out." He flashed Alex a tired smile. "I thought no rangers were allowed over there."

"That rule doesn't apply to me anymore."

For those exciting moments on the dance floor and in her kitchen, it had been just the two of them. No more Kenny. Alex intended things to stay that way from here on out.

Gilly couldn't say no to the chief ranger. She didn't want to.

"I'll be happy to do it." She was thrilled to do it. Since her return from California, she craved Alex's company more and more.

"Thanks, Gilly. You've solved a big problem. As Pierce Gallagher once told me, you are pure gold, but I already knew that."

"Thank you." She hung up the cell phone, dazed by what Jim had just said to her.

The superintendent is elated over the progress Jamal's making under this experimental program. Alex's concern is that Jamal be well looked after. No ranger can do your ranger's job the way you do, but I'm afraid where Jamal's concerned, there isn't another ranger besides you Alex trusts with him.

It's a bit of a dilemma unless we send him back to Indianapolis tomorrow; however Jamal's only supposed to be out here a month. Once his wounds are healed, that time will be about over. I can't see the superintendent bringing him back again.

Neither could Gilly.

Clutching the phone in her hand, she went back in Jamal's bedroom. Alex was standing next to the bed talking quietly to him.

Her body quaked at the sight of his tall, well-honed frame. The bedside lamp highlighted the sunbleached tips of his hair where her fingers had made a foray.

Had the boys noticed her lips which were still slightly swollen from the intensity of his kisses? The feel of his hard body, the pressure of his mouth and the things it had done to her gave new meaning to the term *ecstasy*. She would never be the same again.

When Alex turned his head in her direction, she feared he could see into her psyche and know exactly what she was thinking.

Fortifying herself with a deep breath she said, "Jamal? How would you feel if I take care of you for a while starting tomorrow? And don't tell me 'that'll be cool.' I want the truth!"

He laughed. She could always count on his sense of humor being in evidence.

"What can you cook besides doughnuts?"

She squinted at him. "Frozen meals?"

"I'll make breakfast every morning before I leave for work," Alex volunteered.

Gilly let out an exaggerated sigh to cover the excitement his words engendered. "That's a relief. I think I've got a cookbook stashed somewhere my mother sent me years ago. I've never opened it, but something tells me I'd better go home and find it."

"What for?" Jamal asked with a deadpan expression.

"So you can pick out something you want for dinner and I'll do my best to make it. Deal?"

"But I don't have to promise to eat it. Right?" he teased back.

"Wrong!" She put Alex's phone on the

dresser. "I'll be back in the morning and I expect to find *you* in a repentant mood."

"You sound just like my mom."

Alex's low laughter trailed her down the hall and out the front door of the house. She could still hear it in her mind after she'd gone home to bed.

With almost no sleep the night before, she dropped off the moment her head touched the pillow. When she awakened the next morning, she experienced inexplicable joy to realize she was going to be playing hooky at Alex's house while she took care of Jamal.

After a shower and shampoo, she slipped on jeans, a white T-shirt and sneakers. During the short walk to the house next door, she tried to tamp down those fluttery sensations bombarding her at the thought of seeing Alex.

Even if she'd succeeded, the sight of him flipping pancakes at the stove would have shot her bloodstream with fresh adrenaline. She was so excited, she could hardly contain her feelings

His eyes flashed the color of storm clouds with silver linings. They were beautiful eyes. Extraordinary. This morning they reflected an unusual intensity of emotion, but she couldn't tell where it was coming from.

"You're just in time for breakfast. Sit down at the table and I'll serve these piping hot."

"Jamal's the patient."

"We've already eaten."

Something was wrong. He was saying all the right things, but she could tell he was upset.

"Alex— I didn't come over here for you to wait on me."

"What if I want to?"

"Then thank you."

As soon as she'd taken her place, he brought her a plate that included sausage.

"This looks delicious."

"Let's hope. Coffee?"

"No, thank you."

He poured himself a cup, then sat down opposite her to drink his. They were dressed alike today. His nearness made it difficult for her to function normally, let alone eat.

"Before I leave, you should know Jamal gets a painkiller and antibiotics every four hours. I gave him his first dose at seven. I've made egg salad sandwiches for lunch. They're in the fridge wrapped in foil. The doctor said to press fluids. I picked up Popsicles. He likes those."

Gilly nodded. She was touched by his meticulous care of Jamal.

"If he complains of more pain, I've left the

number of his doctor by the phone over on the counter. Make yourself at home. My computer is at your disposal."

"Thank you, Alex. I'm sure we'll get along fine."

"Knowing you're here for Jamal is all that's important. Larry called me this morning. Since they live so close, Linda will spell you off if you have to leave before four for any reason. I've left their number on the paper, too."

Though Alex had thought of everything, she sensed a definite tension coming from him this morning that hadn't been there last night.

"I'll keep that in mind."

He eyed her narrowly before getting up to put his empty mug in the sink. She watched him reach for his lunch pail.

"Alex?" she called out before he left the kitchen. He paused midstride to look at her. "Out of all the men Jamal could have shadowed, he was fortunate to have been placed with you. I happen to know he knows it, too, otherwise he'd have taken you up on your offer to go back to Indianapolis."

Gilly had wanted to compliment him, but his features unexpectedly formed a grimace. "If he were as lucky as you say he is, he wouldn't be laid up in the bedroom with scalded toes. That was my fault for allowing him too much freedom."

"We've had this discussion before." She got out of the chair. "You weren't asked to be a jailer, and it wasn't his fault Cindy was trying to impress him."

He rubbed the back of his neck restlessly. "Does any of that matter considering the fact that they could have been boiled alive on Dr. Alex Latimer's watch?"

"But they weren't!"

"Quinn Derek expected more from me."

Gilly had no idea he'd taken on so much guilt, but she should have known. "I'm sure Cindy's parents aren't whipping themselves the way you are."

"Then they should be!" he bit out. "As far as I'm concerned, having a child is too damn painful."

"That's your fear talking. You don't mean that."

"The hell I don't."

He left through the garage. For a moment she stood there immobilized. Alex had just allowed her a glimpse into that part of his soul he rarely showed anyone.

At the hospital he'd referred to himself as a wild child. Maybe in time he'd trust her enough to tell her what haunted him.

"Gilly?"

Her eyes darted to the hallway where Jamal was standing with the help of his crutches.

"Jamal— What are you doing up?"

"Alex has been upset all morning."

She could tell the teen was fighting tears. "How much did you hear?"

"Everything."

"Oh, honey—" Without conscious thought she put her arms around him and felt his shoulders heave. "He's not mad at you. His anger proves he loves you."

"He told me he took me on to pay back the grocer who once gave him a chance. I let him down."

"No, Jamal. But it's evident you're the first person he's ever been responsible for in any way. Like every parent with their first child, your accident scared him."

With that comment he laughed a little and raised his head. She wiped the tears off his face with her hand.

"Don't you understand? He got his first taste of what it's like to be a dad. Even I can see it's scary."

"Yeah?"

She nodded. "While he's at work today, he'll calm down. What do you bet he comes home early to see if you're all right."

"It sure didn't sound that way when he left."

"I know, but I bet he does. Come on. Let's get you back on the bed. I've got an idea that might help you with school and make Alex happy at the same time."

After she'd gotten him settled she said, "What would you think if I phoned your high school and asked them to e-mail you a list of your classes for this next year. We could get a head start on your school work while you're lying around recuperating."

"I already know what they'll say. I flunked math."

"Well this is your lucky day because math is easy for me. Maybe if we worked really hard at it, by the time you go home, you could retake the test for a decent grade. What do you think?"

"I never did get math."

"So we'll start from scratch."

She heard him take a big breath. "Okay. I guess we haven't got anything else to do."

"You're terrific. With an attitude like that, you'll probably end up being someone important like Alex."

"You don't want to be like me, Jamal. I'm an idiot."

Gilly let out a soft gasp to realize Alex was

in the doorway of Jamal's room. How long had he been standing there?

The teen showed more composure. His gaze met Gilly's before he said, "What are you doing home?"

"To apologize to both of you. Since I got up, I've been like a bear with a sore head."

"A bear with a sore head?"

The smile that broke out on Alex's face was a miracle. It turned him into the most handsome man alive.

"I don't know where that expression comes from. I've never seen a bear in that condition. I'm not sure I could tell." Jamal grinned. "The point is, I overreacted. Will you forgive me?"

"Sure."

"How about you, Gilly?" His eyes seemed to be searching her very soul.

"Sure," she mimicked Jamal. It was the only way to make it through such an emotional moment without embarrassing herself. "I've been known to overreact myself. Just last night I got scared over something stupid."

Jamal looked fascinated by their exchange. "What?"

"That business about a sniper being on the loose," Alex informed him as if she weren't sitting right there.

"Oh that. You have to figure if that happens, it's your time to go."

She patted Jamal's arm. "It's the only way to look at it."

Alex eyed both of them. "I don't know about you guys, but I feel better. I think I can go to work now."

"You do that," Gilly said in a cheery tone. "We've got work of our own to do." *But be careful, Alex. Come back to me.*

"I heard," Alex admitted without displaying a shred of guilt that he'd eavesdropped. "I'm curious to see how good a math teacher you are."

"Well, once you leave, maybe Jamal can finally find out."

He clamped the teen on the shoulder. "I think Ranger King wants me gone out of my own house."

Jamal looked him in the eye. "I think you're right."

"I told you he wasn't mad," she mouthed the words to Jamal once she was certain Alex had gone.

After finding paper and pen in Alex's study, she returned to begin his first math lesson. In between bathroom, medicine, lunch and snack breaks, he did quite well until they came to fractions and percentages. That's where they would start his lesson the next day.

Gilly urged him to sleep a little while she made enchiladas for their dinner. It was one of the few dishes she couldn't ruin too badly.

In the four days that followed, she discovered Jamal was a pretty good student when he applied himself. They both kept busy with his studies, her painting, visits from friends and a couple of phone calls to Jamal's mother.

Alex usually walked in the house by four-thirty. They played board games and ate dinner before he accompanied her to her front door where she gave him a report of Jamal's progress. There was no news of the sniper. Alex didn't think he'd come to the park.

On the surface everything seemed fine except for one thing. She kept waiting to feel his mouth on hers. Though she saw desire in his eyes when he said good-night, he didn't act on it. Whatever was wrong, it was starting to rip her apart.

On Friday, Gilly got up early and drove Jamal to Jackson to see the doctor. After he'd removed the cast, he declared his toes healed enough to wear shoes and socks again. By the time they got back to the house, Steve was there waiting for Jamal. He'd come dressed in a cowboy hat and sunglasses.

They went in Jamal's room. A few minutes later they came out again. Jamal had put on his Lakers jersey and a baseball cap. "Gilly? Can I have the rest of the day off from doing math?"

He'd been making such good progress, she found herself disappointed by the question, but she tried hard not to show it. Naturally he wanted to celebrate his recovery.

On a deeper level she was in pain because the week was over. She had no more excuse to come and go from Alex's house. She'd give anything to understand why he was keeping his emotional distance from her.

"Gilly?" Jamal prodded.

She blinked.

"Is it okay?"

"Y-yes," she stammered. "Of course. What are you guys going to do?"

"Just mess around at Grant Village," Steve informed her.

Jamal rubbed his hands together. "Look at the ladies."

She rolled her eyes. "That's what I thought."

"Be back for lunch by twelve, otherwise I'll worry."

"I know."

After they took off, she felt such a wrench being left on her own, she got busy doing the dishes and the laundry. Before she gathered up her stuff and moved it back to her house, Jamal's sheets needed changing.

"Bruce? You're in charge. I'm taking today off."

Alex understood the strange look the younger ranger gave him. He'd only been at work ten minutes, just long enough to check the readings and make his notations.

"If you need me, call me on my cell."

"Yes, sir."

Alex had been going hard all week without a break. Before the advent of Gilly who'd come into his life at the same time as Jamal, he wouldn't have given a thought to what time he got back to the cabin he shared with a bunch of other rangers. He'd lived wherever his work had taken him.

But all that had changed when Jim had provided a house where he could live with Jamal for the next month. A house that happened to be next door to the famous number eleven. Since Gilly had been taking care of the teen, Alex found he looked forward to going home at the end of the day.

All he had to do was walk in the kitchen where he could smell something delicious cooking. There she'd be, sketching at his table with an adorable look of concentration on her face. His gaze would take in the voluptuous mold of her body. She'd glance up at him with those startling blue eyes that knocked the breath out of him. At that moment something inside him would expand.

During the short walk to her house in the evening, he would detect the fragrance that came from her silky hair and velvet skin. After giving him a rundown of the day's events with Jamal, she would whisper good-night and slip inside her front door.

Every night the ache for her had been growing. It took all his strength of will not to follow her inside. But he could hardly do that when Jamal was waiting for him. He'd be in bed listening to his radio or writing in his journal. The second he saw Alex, he would pull off his earphones and greet him with a smile. They'd have one of their talks.

In another week the teen would be going back to Indianapolis. Gilly would no longer be living in his house all day. There would be a great void. When he came home after work, there'd be no one there. The thought was insupportable to him.

For that very reason he couldn't leave Norris fast enough to get back to his house. Forty-five minutes later he pulled into his driveway and entered through the front door. His heart banged like a jackhammer.

"Gilly?"

"Alex?" She sounded shocked. "I'm in Jamal's room."

He found her putting clean sheets on the bed. He'd never seen her in shorts before. Her legs were as beautiful as the rest of her.

Her breathing sounded shallow. "What are you doing home?"

"I decided I've worked hard enough this week. Where's Jamal?"

"After his cast came off this morning, he decided he wanted to play, too. Steve drove down from Mammoth. Right now they're over at the marina checking out girls, but they'll be back for lunch."

The last time Alex had glanced at his watch it was ten-thirty. That gave him a good hour to be alone with this woman who had a stranglehold on him without even trying.

He moved over to the bed and started to help her by fitting the corners of the flat sheet on his side.

"Thank you," she murmured, avoiding his eyes.

As she started to throw on the top sheet, he

caught it and tugged, causing her to lose her balance so they both landed on the bed with her body halfway on top of him. A little cry of surprise came from her throat.

"It's time you had a rest from your duties as well," he whispered against her lips before claiming them possessively.

He'd been living for this.

The memory of her last response was all that had been keeping him going. Bursting with needs he could no longer suppress, he rolled her over to drink deeply from that heart shaped mouth he couldn't get enough of. No woman had such a mouth, or eyes, or hair, or skin.

"You're so incredibly beautiful." He pressed kisses to her hot cheek and temple. "When I first saw you, I could hardly believe you were real.

"I want you, Gilly, and I know you want me," his voice throbbed. "Even if you can't say the words, a man knows when a woman feels this kind of desire for him."

"I'm not denying it," she whispered. "But all week you've kept your distance from me."

"You have to know why," he murmured against her lips. "One taste of you and I forget everything else. With Jamal expecting my attention, I haven't dared touch you. But he's not here now and there's no place I want to be except with you."

"I think I willed you to come home early," she admitted breathlessly.

He cried her name before they started giving each other kiss for kiss. What started out as playful teasing soon changed to something else as their hunger escalated. With the passing of time no kiss seemed long enough or deep enough. He buried his face in her scented neck.

"I want to make love to you, sweetheart, but I realize this isn't the place or the time. Any second now Jamal will come bursting in with Steve, so let's have an understanding here and now."

"What understanding?" she cried softly, kissing his jaw before pressing her mouth to his once more. They couldn't begin to get enough of each other.

"When it's time to put Jamal on the plane, we'll drive him to Salt Lake and then we'll fly to Vancouver Island. Have you ever been there?"

"No," she half moaned the word as he proceeded to devour her once more.

When he eventually came up for air he said, "I know a place that will delight you. It's a little cabin by the ocean in a spot so remote most people don't know about it." That's where he'd yearned to take her from the very beginning.

"We'll ask for two weeks off for ourselves. The last thing I want to do is hurry this with you. We need whole days and nights of loving in total privacy. No deadlines, no worries. Just each other. I've been living for it. Jim will let us have the time together."

Feverish with longing, he sought her mouth once more, wishing they were already there. She fit so perfectly in his arms. He turned on his back and pulled her around so he could feel her on top of him once more.

At first she was with him all the way, then inexplicably she tore her mouth from his and raised up, using his shoulders for leverage. Looking down at him from anguished blue eyes she said, "I'm not sure that would be a good idea, Alex."

"Give me one reason why."

"It's…too soon." Her voice shook.

"If this is about your husband, I know you loved him and always will. But just now you were responding to me and only me."

Her eyes closed tightly. "This has nothing to with Kenny."

He covered her face with kisses. "I know there isn't another man, Gilly," he ground out. "So what's wrong?"

"I just think we need to get to know each other better before we…go off together."

"Why?" he demanded, extracting another kiss from her mouth that brought them both rapture and left them trembling with unassuaged needs. "What we feel for each other doesn't come along very often, if ever."

"I-I agree. It's for that reason we shouldn't rush it."

She was hiding something from him, but he didn't know what. Her unexpected hesitation cooled his blood faster than an arctic blast. He didn't try to stop her when she slid off him and stood up.

"I'll start lunch for everyone."

While she disappeared out the door, Alex lay there in a stupor. He recalled a certain conversation she'd had with Jamal to clear up the initial misunderstanding between them.

Well, for the last week that guy has been hounding me to go out on a date with him. I told him no, but he's the kind of man who doesn't care what a woman wants or doesn't want.

His thoughts flew back to certain things Jim had confided in him about the demented ranger who'd stalked her at Teton Park. Maybe Jim hadn't told him everything.

Good Lord.

If she'd been physically assaulted, it might explain her fear of intimacy.

In an instant he'd levered himself from the bed.

If that were the case, then the experience with the construction worker must have terrified her. Alex groaned to think that, because of her fears, she might ever put Alex in the same category.

Gilly wanted him. There'd been no mistaking the signs, but she hadn't been able to let herself go. Especially when he'd talked about taking her away someplace.

Was that when she'd suddenly felt helpless? Powerless?

They needed to talk. He had to find out if what he was thinking was true.

She wasn't going anywhere. Once Alex knew the truth, then he'd find a way to get her to open up to him.

His happiness depended on it.

After making up the rest of Jamal's bed, he walked through the house to the kitchen where she was emptying a sack of potato chips into a bowl. He helped by putting the plate of sandwiches on the table.

"Gilly?"

She lifted her head. When he saw the shadows in her eyes, pain stabbed his gut repeatedly to think he might have frightened her. He needed to repair the damage fast.

"Did that ranger hurt you, is that why you're scared?"

CHAPTER EIGHT

ALEX's question was so way off base, Gilly realized he truly didn't know what was wrong.

She'd been on the verge of giving heart, mind, soul and body to him. But Jamal's accident had caused a certain admission to come out of Alex. He didn't want children. Did that mean he didn't want marriage, either? Knowing that had helped her step away from a line she'd almost crossed.

The Alex Latimers of this world only came along once in a lifetime, but you didn't tie a man like him down. He'd had to claw his way through his formative years on his own power. So far he hadn't allowed himself to need another person, and had told her so last night.

As long as no word of love had passed his lips, she wasn't about to divulge her love for him, let alone act on that love by going away with him. She'd lost someone she loved once, she couldn't put herself through that again.

"No," she proclaimed at last. "Chief Gallagher had me transferred to Yellowstone before anything like that could happen."

"Thank God."

"I have. Many times."

She couldn't sustain Alex's piercing glance any longer. "As long as you're home, there are things I need to do. Jamal will be thrilled when he comes in and realizes you're here. Now if you'll excuse me—"

Without hesitation she left him sitting there and hurried back to her own house where she could be alone with her thoughts.

It had killed her to turn him down, but she couldn't begin to imagine the pain if she'd agreed to take a vacation with him. Once their passionate interlude was over, it would be business as usual.

Gilly might not know any of the women who'd loved him before now, but when he'd walked away from them, she knew he'd left every single one of them *devastated.*

After two years of grieving for her husband, she wasn't about to risk her whole adult life being destroyed by a one-sided love that had no future. She could never have an affair with a man. Yet if she gave into her craving for Alex one more time, that was where her relationship with him was headed.

Since Jamal was back on his feet, she no longer had an excuse to be a part of Alex's life. In another week Jamal would be going back to Indianapolis, leaving Alex in an empty house. Not only would it be torture for her to continue living next door to him, it would be foolish.

He'd either drop by her place, or ask her to drop by his when he wanted some loving, but there'd be no strings. No promises. No commitment. He wasn't capable of it where a woman was concerned. Otherwise he'd have been married by now.

Gilly had to remember he'd told her he could never handle being a father. At the time she hadn't wanted to believe him, just thought he was scared, not ready, but she was beginning to now.

Unfortunately she'd fallen madly in love with him. He was the man she wanted to be her husband and the father of her children. But since that wasn't a possibility, then they'd reached a permanent stalemate.

The more she thought about it, the more she realized that every chance meeting with him from now on would destroy her a little more. If she moved to another part of the park to work, it still wouldn't help. He would dominate her every thought. She couldn't put herself through the pain.

Yellowstone wasn't big enough for both of them. Neither was the State of Wyoming! Since Jim had been forced to find other rangers to do her job this last week, maybe now would be the best time to consider a transfer.

With her mind made up, she went into her study and turned on the computer. For the next little while she looked over the possibilities, then e-mailed applications for employment to the chief rangers at Yosemite, Joshua Tree, Sequoia, Kings Canyon and Redwood parks in California.

No matter their response, she would give Jim her two weeks' notice right now. If a job didn't become available by the time she left the park, she could always stay with her parents until one did.

Settling down to her task, she e-mailed her letter of resignation to him with the explanation that she was missing her family too much and wanted to move closer to home.

With that accomplished, she felt better about the steps she'd taken to leave Yellowstone for good. Her future with Kenny had been cut off too soon, yet because of Alex she'd found out the spirit was resilient. Being around Jamal made her realize she wanted to try for another baby.

However it would require a change in location in order to meet the right man. No man would ever be Alex of course. No man would ever thrill her the same way again. It wasn't possible.

Still, there were other things to look for. Perhaps in time her future would be filled with a husband and children, but not if she stayed here languishing after Alex whose vision was far different from hers.

Unable to stay alone in the house with her torturous thoughts another second, Gilly packed an overnight bag and headed for the garage. It was after two. Sydney would be on duty at Old Faithful until four. Gilly would find her friend and stick with her for the weekend.

Using the remote on the Toyota visor to open the garage door, she started to back out.

"Gilly?" a familiar male voice called to her, causing her heart to jump in its cavity. She turned her head in Alex's direction.

He came striding toward her with a concerned look on his striking features. "Have you heard from Jamal?"

"No— Didn't they come home for lunch?"

His brows furrowed. "Afraid not. Both their

cell phones have been turned off. I drove over to the marina to get them, but they weren't anywhere around. Larry has alerted all the rangers to be on the lookout for them."

"Maybe they went out on the lake and lost track of the time."

"I checked. They didn't rent a boat. Steve's folks are clueless about his plans. Right now Bob's searching the north end of the park. His wife is looking around Gardiner for any sign of the Honda."

Gilly felt a pit in her stomach that was growing bigger by the second. When she saw the same worry in Alex's eyes that had been there the night they'd rushed to Jamal's side at the hospital, she was sick at heart and riddled with fresh guilt.

"I should never have told him he could leave the house, but he was so happy to have the cast removed, I thought it would be—"

"Don't blame yourself for something that's not your fault," he ordered in a fierce tone. "What I need to know is, was it Steve's or Jamal's idea to be together today?"

"I don't know for certain. When we got back from Jackson, Steve was waiting for Jamal. They both have cell phones and could have planned to meet ahead of time. As for whose idea it was to get together, it's anyone's guess."

A nerve pulsed at the corner of the mouth that had kissed her senseless earlier. "Bob tells me Steve manages to get into trouble on a regular basis. Jamal likes him, which would make it hard for him to turn Steve down even if he's up to something he shouldn't be doing."

His eyes closed for a minute. "I was hoping there'd be no more episodes before I put him on the plane back to his mother."

Alex stood close enough she saw the shudder that rocked his hard body. She could feel his alarm because it was an extension of her own. The idea that a sniper might still be loose in the area lurked in both their minds, but she didn't want to think about that right now.

Without conscious thought she said, "I'll help you look for him."

"We'll take my car."

She nodded before driving her car back in the garage. After plucking her binoculars from the truck, she emerged to discover he'd already pulled the Explorer into her driveway and had opened the door for her. Once she'd climbed in, they took off for the marina.

"I've been thinking, Alex. They've both got a crush on Syd and might be hanging out at the junior rangers' clubhouse. I'll call her and tell her to take a look inside, just in case."

"Good idea," Alex muttered, but she could tell his fears for Jamal's safety had taken over. The memory of the accident at the thermal pool was still fresh in both their minds.

After making the call, she put the binoculars to her eyes and scanned the sea of cars while Alex drove back and forth. After ten minutes with no success, she lowered them to her lap. One glance at him and she noticed the deep lines of stress bracketing his mouth.

"Alex, since the rangers are actively searching for them, why don't we drive to West Yellowstone. If the boys are doing something wrong, I've a feeling they're not going to risk getting caught within the park boundaries."

"You're probably right. By now they could be halfway to Salt Lake."

"Maybe Steve got on the Internet and is going to buy another games console to replace the one his dad took away."

"It's a possibility." He pulled out his cell phone. "I'll alert the sheriff and ask him to put out an APB on the Honda."

During the hour it took to reach West Yellowstone, they both used binoculars to scan the terrain while they made more calls. By the time Alex pulled in front of a store that sold electronic games, she'd spoken to both Beth and

Sydney. Neither had seen the teens, but they assured her they'd start their own search.

Alex levered himself from the car. Before closing the door he said, "I'll be right back. I want to find out if the boys have been here."

She nodded and kept her eyes trained on the traffic for any sign of them. When he came out a few minutes later, his grim expression left nothing to the imagination.

Gilly's heart pained her to see him in this kind of agony. "Let's drive around to all the places the kids their age like to hang out. Maybe they're at the movies or the bowling alley."

Before she knew it, night had fallen, making the search more difficult. They'd covered literally every inch of road without discovering a clue to the boys' whereabouts. The constant checks with Larry and Steve's parents who were frantic with concern increased her feelings of helplessness and panic.

It wasn't just Jamal's disappearance that frightened her. Alex was in a special kind of hell.

After eating at a drive-through she said, "It's just an idea, but maybe Steve wanted to show Jamal around before he has to fly home. I heard them talking about the Mesa Falls marathon Steve's going to run in August."

Without saying anything Alex headed south out of town. He didn't pull off the highway again until they reached the turnoff for the Hebgen Lake Road. Fewer cars were out on the road now. As each one passed, she prayed it would be the Honda.

When Alex turned to her, she didn't recognize his eyes. Their color had grown dark as pitch. "I don't doubt your hunch could be inspired, but the fact that they haven't checked in with anyone after this long leads me to believe they're met up with trouble not necessarily of their own making."

"If that's true, Jamal can take care of himself," she declared with more confidence than she felt. "He's told me a few tales. I've decided he's been a lot wilder than you were growing up."

She heard his sharp intake of breath. "You're wrong about that, Gilly. He has a mother who's always loved and tempered him to some degree."

"Meaning you lost yours early in life?" The question came out before she could stop it.

"In a way."

Gilly bit her lip. "I don't understand. Tell me about your family, Alex. I've always wondered why you haven't mentioned them. So many times I've wanted to ask, but because you never volunteered any information, I was afraid you would think I was prying."

His mouth tautened. "There's not a lot to tell since I don't have a clue who even fathered me. In case you're tempted to ask me about my mother, I haven't seen her since I was six years old."

"Six?" she cried softly.

"That's right. I have no idea where she is today."

"Oh Alex—"

"According to one social worker, she had too many boyfriends and ended up neglecting me, so I was taken away from her early."

Gilly groaned in pain.

"If she loved me, she never tried to find me. I grew up going from one foster home to another."

In one breath, Alex had painted a picture of his past life she would never have imagined. One foster home after another? Her heart bled for the boy inside the remarkable man who'd never known the love of his own parents. Her eyes stung with tears.

"You can't imagine that can you," his voice grated.

She shook her head, fighting to get control

of her emotions. Later when she was home and could give in to her feelings, she would sob her heart out for the family he'd been deprived of growing up.

Gilly had always taken her own family for granted. She couldn't relate to Alex's life.

"To have to make it to adulthood without loving parents or siblings is anathema to me," she admitted.

"I kept hoping my mother would come for me. Every single day I waited. When it never happened, I'm afraid I became pretty impossible to control. I resented anyone who tried to get close to me.

"Nobody was going to tell me what to do but my parents, and since mine weren't around, I refused to tolerate anyone else."

"I don't blame you for feeling that way."

"You can say that now, but at the time I got into a lot of trouble with the police for stealing cars and ripping off stuff from stores. One of the social workers found me a job at a neighborhood grocery store. It was my last chance to shape up. If I didn't, then no one would bail me out of juvenile detention the next time. It was hard, Gilly, really hard.

"But Mr. Wicks, the old man who owned the store, didn't lay down any laws, or try to father me. All he said was, "You can blow it and end up in prison for the rest of your life, or you can do a good job here and get paid real money for it. If you do it well, I'll give you bonuses.

"I liked it that he left me alone and didn't come off trying to be my friend. He never asked any questions, never bugged me. In fact he was a tough old guy. Over time I started bugging him because he came to work early, and went home late. I found out he'd lost his entire family years earlier in a car crash and had lived alone ever since."

"That poor man."

"In a way, he was like me. He didn't have anyone else, either. I found out he'd been a chemical engineer before his only brother died, leaving the grocery store to run. Little by little we became friends. He was the reason I finished high school and went to college. The rest, as you say, is history."

Gilly wiped the tears dripping off her chin. "Is he still alive?"

"No, he passed away a month before I received my Ph.D. Would you believe he left me everything in his will?"

"Yes!" she cried. "He believed in you the same way you've believed in Jamal."

With this revelation she understood so much

better his fierce defense of the teen. When Alex had thought she'd rejected the boy, no doubt he'd been remembering his own feelings of rejection. The deprivations of his own childhood would make him understand more than most people what a boy like Jamal had to deal with knowing his father was in prison.

Alex had obviously been blessed with a wonderful brain, but that alone hadn't turned him into such a remarkable human being. In spite of the greatest kind of adversity, maybe even because of it, he'd managed to make a triumph of his life.

After what he'd just revealed, to tell him how much she admired him would sound like a meaningless platitude.

He obviously thought he'd said enough because he started up the car and they began driving through the forest.

"I should never have agreed to let Jamal shadow me," he bit out, pounding the heel of his hand against the steering wheel. "His mother trusted me to take care of him. I thought I could be his Mr. Wicks, but Jamal has his own demons that are driving him right now. If something has happened to him…"

"Don't, Alex!" She put a hand on his arm. "He's around here somewhere. I know he'll show up."

"Can you promise me that?"

His agony was so great, she didn't know how to reach him. "No, but I refuse to believe that someone as wonderful and generous as you will be required to go through any more suffe—"

Just then Alex's cell phone rang, cutting off the rest of her words. He reached for it. "It's the sheriff!"

Gilly held her breath while Alex clicked on. She didn't have to wait long to know something earthshaking had happened. Suddenly they were racing down the highway, breaking the speed limit.

Alex put the phone on the seat. "The police just found Jamal and Steve breaking in to some guy's truck at the Island Park motel. That's not far from here."

"Thank heaven they're alive, Alex! I don't care about anything else right now."

He reached over and grabbed hold of her hand. "Neither do I. Unfortunately they're in big trouble."

"Then there has to be an explanation! Jamal loves you too much to do something this stupid."

"Love?" he mocked in self-abnegation before putting his other hand back on the wheel. "Don't kid yourself. Jamal sees any adult as the enemy. I know how his mind works because I've been there and done it all.

"Since he was laid up, he's been marking time until he could go home. When Bob hears about this, he's going to rue the day his son got involved with Jamal. No doubt he was trying to impress Steve by ripping off a stereo and anything else worth money. I'm afraid this is one plan the governor won't try to implement again, no matter how worthy."

"Don't jump to conclusions yet, Alex."

He flashed her an impatient glance. "It's the mother in you that wants to believe in Jamal."

"It's the father in you that's too upset right now to be thinking clearly!" she fired back.

"Father—"

"Yes. That's what you've been to him. He waits for you to come home. He lights up every time you walk in the door. It's Alex this, and Alex that. He thinks you walk on water. That's why I'm positive there's something else going on here."

"I hope to God you're right," he muttered as they passed the sign for Island Park. Inside of a minute they saw half a dozen police cars with their lights flashing outside the motel. The Honda was parked between a couple of SUVs.

The police had put up barricades to keep everyone away.

Alex flashed one of the officers his ID and they were let through. He drove them over to the sheriff's car and got out. Gilly jumped to the ground, then cringed when she caught sight of the two teens in handcuffs, lined up against another police car. She moved closer to Alex.

The sheriff approached them. "I presume you're Dr. Latimer." Alex nodded. "I've notified Ranger Carr. He and his wife are on their way."

Alex nodded. "Tell me what happened."

"One of the patrons at the motel noticed the teens skulking around and called us when they saw them lifting the tarp off that rig over there."

Gilly looked over at the white truck. It was pulling a trailer loaded with a twenty-one-foot boat.

"Where's the owner of the rig?"

"She's in the police car over there giving information to the officers. She's going to press charges."

"What's the boy's explanation?" Alex clipped out.

"The one in the baseball cap and Lakers shirt told the other one to be quiet, insisting they had nothing to say except to you or an attorney."

Gilly's eyes met Alex's. Jamal had been in trouble so many times, he knew what to do in a situation like this. In spite of the circumstances, she couldn't help but give Alex a faint smile.

He turned to the sheriff. "If it's all right, I'd like to talk to them."

"Go ahead."

"Come on," Alex whispered to Gilly, putting a hand behind her neck to guide her.

A couple of officers stood guard. One of them told the boys they could turn around.

When they glimpsed Alex and Gilly, she thought she'd see relief on their faces. Their stoic reaction wasn't at all what she'd expected. If they'd been doing something wrong, they displayed no guilt, no cowering.

"Hello, Jamal," Alex said before nodding to Steve. "What's been going on since Gilly said you could spend an hour at the marina?"

"We've been on junior ranger business."

That sounded like a code to Gilly. Alex must have thought the same thing because his hand bit into her shoulder. He didn't know his own strength, but she didn't mind. She loved him beyond caution.

Jamal squinted up at him. "Can I talk to you in private?"

"Sure."

He let go of Gilly and moved closer to Jamal so the teen could whisper to him.

"You know that woman in the cop car over there?"

"What about her?" Alex whispered back.

"She's the sniper. Only I'm positive she's a man, not a woman. You've got to stop him quick."

Alex blinked. "Do you have proof?"

"Yeah. That truck's been painted white, but it's blue underneath. Pull off the engine cover of the inboard. Instead of an engine you'll find a slug of firearms and ammo. He's got a PSG 1 silence sniper rifle, but it's in parts."

Good Lord.

"This has got to be the truth, Jamal."

"Please trust me?"

Maybe he and Steve had caught the sniper, maybe not. But a stash of guns hidden beneath an engine cover was reason enough to arrest him.

"I'll be right back."

Alex walked over to Gilly whose faith in Jamal so far was absolute. He'd never known such an amazing woman. Much as he wanted to answer all the questions blazing in those gorgeous blue eyes, he couldn't take the time right now.

"Stay with the boys." He gave her shoulder a squeeze before approaching the sheriff.

"Since Jamal's been in my care, I'm his official guardian. Mind if I talk to the owner of the rig?"

"Go ahead."

As he walked over to one of the officers standing by the police car, his adrenaline flew off the charts. "Hi. I'm Dr. Alex Latimer, the head ranger from the Yellowstone Volcano Observatory. Jamal Carter has been shadowing me for his careers class. The sheriff has given me permission to talk to the woman whose rig the boys were vandalizing. Would you ask her to step out of the car and away from it, please?"

"Sure."

All Alex saw was a lean looking woman with short, dark red hair. It was a solid red. She was wearing jeans with an oversize T-shirt that fell over her straight hips. When the tall woman climbed out of the car, there was nothing feminine about her body language.

His gaze fell to her hand and forearm. They looked whipcord strong. Like a man's.

All Alex had to go on was Jamal's word and Gilly's faith in the teen. That had to be enough, because what he was about to do next could land him in jail.

Using one of the same street moves he'd pulled on the construction worker, he threw him to the ground, pinning the man's arms behind his back. Alex rejoiced to see the red wig come off, revealing a bald-headed guy who looked close to thirty years of age.

"Get the cuffs on him," Alex shouted. "This guy could be the sniper. Sheriff? There's a pile of weapons under the engine cover of the boat. Call Ranger Smith and he'll inform the FBI agents working on this case."

Everyone scrambled to do their job. Alex left the man writhing ineffectually on the ground to join Gilly and the boys. The three of them stared at him like he'd just grown another head.

He turned to one of the officers. "Mind taking those cuffs off my boys? They're the park's best junior rangers and have been working undercover for us."

The officer grinned. "It would be an honor."

Once they were free, Jamal put out his hand to high-five Alex, but Alex's emotions were running too high. He grabbed Jamal around the waist and gave him a bear hug that lifted him off the ground. When he glanced at Gilly, she was hugging Steve for all he was worth.

Before long the place was swarming with agents. Soon Steve's parents arrived and statements were taken. By the time Jamal and Steve were free to go home, it was almost midnight.

Steve ended up driving with his mom in the Honda. Gilly walked Jamal to the Explorer where he climbed in back, waiting for Alex to join them.

Agent Montoya caught up to him before he reached the car. "We'll send everything to forensics, but I believe we've got our sniper thanks to Jamal."

"He couldn't have done it without Steve's help."

The other man smiled. "Something tells me Jamal would have found a way."

Something told Alex the same thing. As he reached the car, he realized life wouldn't be worth living without the two people seated inside. When Gilly turned around and smiled at him, he felt like his universe had just opened up to wonders he'd never known were there before.

"Okay," she said once he'd climbed behind the wheel. "Now that you're here, Jamal's going to tell us everything from the beginning. Don't you dare leave anything out."

Jamal laughed. It was music to Alex's ears. Earlier tonight his thoughts had been so black, he'd been afraid he might never seen the boy alive again.

"Steve and I decided to try and help find the sniper, so we drove around Grant Village looking at all the trucks. We knew the police were looking for a red or blue truck with Idaho plates, but anyone can change the paint so I looked at all of them that had Idaho plates.

"There was this white one. Before the woman got back in the truck, she changed the plates to Arizona plates. When she opened the door, the end of it was blue, not white. Because the woman driving it looked like a man to me, I told Steve to follow her. We ended up at Fishing Bridge."

Gilly exchanged stunned glances with Alex.

"The woman got out and locked the cab. But the second she disappeared in one of the stores, I sneaked under the boat tarp for a look around. Steve kept watch. If the woman came back before I could get out, he'd phone me and I'd stay put until the next stop.

"I didn't see anything in the back, but I remembered hearing some of my street buddies talking about the way drugs are smuggled into the country. Sometimes they do it in a boat with no engine.

"So I went over to the engine cover and sure enough underneath were all these guns. Steve told me the woman was coming, so I lay on the floor. He followed until we reached the motel. When the woman went inside, he phoned me and I climbed out. I guess that's when someone saw us and phoned the police."

"You could have been killed!" Gilly cried.

Alex echoed her cry.

"We weren't thinking about that. It was fun. Especially when we saw the way you took out that guy in one move." He sat forward to pat Alex's shoulder.

She stared hard at Alex. "That was pretty spectacular," she said before looking at Jamal. "How did you know it was a man?"

He made a funny sound in his throat. "You've got to be one to know the difference. It's in the way they smile and move and breathe. You could never pretend to be a man, Gilly."

The breath expelled from Alex's lungs. He glanced at her and noticed a faint blush on her cheeks. "You got that right, Jamal."

'I bet you're starving," she interjected.

Alex smiled to himself. "Do you want to stop in West Yellowstone for a meal, Jamal?"

"No. I'd rather go home and eat your bacon and eggs. They're the best."

Gilly eyed Alex intently. "Did you hear that?"

He nodded. His throat had swelled with emotion for so many reasons, he couldn't articulate right now.

CHAPTER NINE

DURING the ride to West Yellowstone, Gilly interjected comments at appropriate intervals while Alex and Jamal talked about the experience they'd just lived through.

But she was still reacting to the fact both Jamal and Steve, certainly Alex, could have been killed tonight. She had no doubts the man dressed as a woman carried a handgun, but Alex's moves had been too expert and swift for him to react.

Gilly would never forget how terrified Alex was that something unspeakable might have happened to Jamal today. After the accident at the thermal pool, his deepest feelings had become involved.

It was probably a good thing Jamal would be returning to Indianapolis shortly. Heaven forbid if something else happened to the teen beforehand. Alex would be torn apart. His confidence shattered.

Until he left, Gilly intended to keep Jamal around no matter how restless he became. He could come to work with her if he wanted. She would cook him more doughnuts, anything to make certain he went home safely to his mother.

While she was still pondering the traumatic events of the night, Alex slowed down at the entrance to the park. Larry had spotted them and stepped out of the ranger station to talk.

He walked over to Jamal's side of the car and rapped on the window so he'd put it down. With a smile on his face he said, "Let me be the first to congratulate you, Jamal."

The boy darted Alex a questioning glance before looking back at the ranger. "What are you talking about?"

"You caught the sniper. Even without the ballistics report, the fingerprints related to another case are a match."

"Cool!"

Larry threw back his head and laughed. "It's very cool. The guy's in the country without papers. He's wanted in Canada. Everybody's happy he's been caught. With him on the loose, the parks have already been losing money. You did a great thing, son.

"Any day now you'll be hearing from the chief, but I wanted you to know right now you've done something the whole country will thank you for. On behalf of every ranger in the park, I'd like to shake your hand. It's an honor to know you, Jamal."

"Steve helped me."

"I know, but you were the one with the instincts only a few men possess. They're something you to have to be born with."

Gilly's tear-filled eyes happened to meet Alex's. She thought his glistened, too, but she couldn't be certain. If the two of them were Jamal's parents, she doubted they could be any prouder.

"Thanks, Larry." Alex's voice sounded husky. "Let's go home, everybody."

When they pulled in his garage a few minutes later Jamal turned to Gilly after she'd climbed out. "Do you have to go home yet?"

Her heart pounded out of rhythm at the thought of spending any more time tonight in Alex's presence. She shouldn't do it, but it was Jamal who was asking. Alex stood next to the teen saying nothing.

"What did you have in mind?"

"I don't know. Just chill for a while."

She bit her lip. "After you captured the sniper that has paralyzed everyone, I guess no one deserves the right to debrief more than you do. I'll come in for a few minutes, but only if you lie down on the bed and elevate your foot."

"It's fine."

"I'll be the judge of that."

"Yes, ma'am."

As they filed through the house she said, "That expression makes me feel old."

"When I first saw you on the street in West Yellowstone, I thought you were only a couple of years older than me."

"Is that right."

"That's why I whistled at you."

"I think everyone in Montana heard it."

He grinned. By now they'd reached his room. "Off with your shoes and socks."

Once Jamal had settled back on the bed, she and Alex took a peek. "You're right," she said. "The skin is peeling and there's no infection."

"The good news is, I can still count five toes," Alex commented.

Jamal laughed. So did Gilly.

When Alex joined in, it touched her heart. She never thought to hear that sound come out of him again. Filled with emotions breaking through the surface, she sat down on the side of the bed.

"Are you honestly all right, honey?"

"Yeah. You two are acting all weird."

"That's because we love you and have been worried sick about you. You don't even want to know all the bad things we were thinking when we couldn't find you. What if you were in trouble, and needed help? What if Alex hadn't reached you in time to stop that man?"

He sobered. "I guess I put you guys in danger, huh."

"Forget that," Alex muttered. "What you did means many lives have been spared."

"Most people think I'm no good like my father."

"That shows you how much they know. He gave your mom a son any mother on earth would love to call her own." She kissed his forehead, then got up from the bed. "Now you need to eat and go to bed. I'll see you later."

If she didn't get out of there now, she was going to break down sobbing. The conversation had become too painful because she loved both these men and was going to lose them.

Alex accompanied her to the front door. He stood there with his powerful legs slightly apart. "There's something I need to ask you before you leave."

She folded her arms to stop the trembling. "What is it?"

"What would you think if I invited Jamal to stay with me for the rest of the summer?"

Gilly's breath caught. It appeared Alex was willing to risk more worry to keep Jamal around after all. Naturally she was happy about that. But for a brief moment she'd thought he was going to ask or tell her something personal that would light up her world.

"I have no idea if Jamal would want to," Alex continued when she didn't say anything. "And even if he did, I might be setting him up for some bigger disappointment down the road. Naturally I'd have to talk it over with his mother.

"Since you've gotten close to him and have a woman's perspective, I'd like your opinion."

For a man who'd never needed anyone to survive, it seemed Jamal had changed him. Obviously they were good for each other. If Gilly didn't love Jamal so much, she'd be jealous of his place in Alex's life. Being loved by him was no small thing.

But Alex was right. There were a lot of factors to consider. Jamal's welfare had to come first.

She cleared her throat. "Since his accident I've been thinking about how nice it would be if his mother and sister could come and stay a few days after his time is up. I think that would tell you a lot."

His lids veiled his eyes. "I'd considered that. Now that you've reinforced the idea, I think it's a good plan. Thank you."

"You're welcome."

"Are you going to be all right tonight?"

Her head flew back. "Why wouldn't I be?"

"Sometimes when shock wears off, we feel vulnerable. Just remember I'm next door if you need me."

"I'll be fine. Even if Jamal has a lot of wisdom in him and is years older than Steve in some ways, he's going to need you tonight."

The whole time they'd been talking, she could feel the energy between them. It was growing stronger and deeper. They were saying one thing with their mouths, but their bodies were saying something else, wanting something else.

On her way out the door she paused and looked back at him. "I admire you more than you can imagine, Alex. You're the finest man I know. It was my luck when Ranger Latimer moved into number ten. You've come to my rescue more than once. That's not something I'm going to forget."

His well-shaped brows, the same dark blond

as his hair, suddenly furrowed. Those silvery eyes turned to flint. "You sound like you're giving a going away speech."

Gilly supposed she was. She should have been more careful. "I've been wanting to compliment you for quite a while. After what happened tonight, I couldn't hold back. For once in your life why don't you try to accept it graciously."

If she'd slapped him, he couldn't have looked more surprised.

"Is it that hard for you?"

He rubbed his chest unconsciously. "Until now I didn't know it was," he ground out.

"Jamal has the same problem, only he's not quite the hard-core case you are yet. He at least smiles while he's deflecting one. I repeat. You're a wonderful man."

"Gilly—"

The way he said her name turned her bones to liquid.

"Yes?"

She felt the shudder that rocked his hard body. He couldn't say the words she needed to hear. In the next instant she ran out on the porch and down the steps to her house, hoping to make it inside before she collapsed in agony.

* * *

"Well, Mrs. King? Do you think you'd like working here at Sequoia?"

Chief Ranger Meeks couldn't have been nicer during her interview. "It would be a privilege. Are there many applicants?"

"A half-dozen. The job has been open for about three weeks. After one more I'll make my decision. Are you looking anywhere else?"

"A position has just opened up at Joshua Tree National Park, but I haven't interviewed there yet."

"It's a wonderful place, but Sequoia has more of a variety of experiences to offer." Until now he hadn't said anything to try to pressure her one way or the other. He had a laid-back personality she liked very much.

"I'm sure you're right."

"I can tell you haven't made up your mind yet. Go back to Yellowstone and think about it some more. If you decide this is what you want, e-mail my office right away so I can start the elimination process. There are two other rangers who want the position badly."

"I understand." She got to her feet. "Thank you so much for seeing me." They shook hands before she left Park Headquarters and drove away from Ash Mountain in her rental car.

Because she'd eaten lunch with him and

other key personnel, she didn't have to make any stops during the two-hour drive to Fresno where she would catch the return flight to Salt Lake. From there she'd fly back to West Yellowstone.

Determined to accomplish all of it on her day off, she'd left home at six this morning. By the time she drove in her driveway, it would 10:00 p.m.

As the hours passed and she made her connecting flights, she discovered she wasn't any closer to a decision than before she'd left for California.

The giant sequoia trees were spectacular. It was an awesome world of steep canyons and breathtaking scenery. She'd be so much closer to her parents' home in Del Mar.

Yet to her chagrin she didn't feel the same pull that had attracted her to the Tetons and Yellowstone. Over time both parks had become pretty inseparable in her mind.

She had to remember that when she'd applied for the forest ranger job, she'd been searching for a new life. When she'd been offered a position with Chief Gallagher, she'd been glad to have been assigned there. It meant she could get going in her career in order to find herself.

This time everything was different. She was running from a man.

As she discovered today, it didn't matter how many miles she put between herself and Alex, she would never be able to stop thinking about him, aching for him.

Looking up at those enormous sequoias had given her such a lonely feeling, she couldn't get away from them fast enough.

When her plane touched down at the small airport, West Yellowstone had never looked as good to her. She got in her Toyota and headed for the park with a feeling of homecoming so strong it overwhelmed her.

By the time she entered the Old Faithful area, her emotions were in chaos. She found herself driving straight to Sydney's cabin. Luckily her friend was still up.

"I don't know what to do, Syd." She stood in the middle of the living room with her face buried in her hands. "I can't stay here, but there's no way I could work at Sequoia. Not when I'm feeling like this."

"Then just go home to Del Mar."

"I couldn't live with my parents again."

"I meant get yourself an apartment. Maybe you ought to go back to school and become an attorney like your mom and brother. With your smarts you'd pass the LSAT in a shot. Studying might be one way to help you get over Alex."

Law school?

"The thought never entered my head."

"I know. Maybe that's a good enough reason to try. You've already got your undergraduate degree. Why don't you stay with me tonight and we'll talk about it."

She glanced at Sydney. "If you don't mind, I think I'll take you up on your offer."

"I was hoping you'd say that. Tomorrow we can sleep in and then go to that ceremony they're planning for Jamal at headquarters."

"Alex was hoping his mother and sister would fly out, but yesterday after work, Jamal came over to tell me his mom wouldn't be comfortable about coming here with so many strangers."

"I guess he knows his mother best." Gilly nodded. "Why don't you get your bag out of the car while I make us some treats."

"Sounds good."

Feeling the way she did right now, it would be too painful to drive home knowing Alex was next door. If she happened to see him, she feared she'd lose any self-control she had left and invite him inside.

Once he'd crossed over her threshold, that

would be it. Then that horrid old adage would come to pass. *Indulge now, repent at leisure.*

Gilly shook her head. She couldn't risk momentary fulfillment followed by a lifetime of emptiness. She just couldn't.

While Jamal was talking to some of the rangers in the conference room at headquarters, Alex stepped down the hall to Jim's office. He tapped on the glass, bringing the chief's head up.

"Have you got a minute before the meeting gets started?"

Jim took one look at him and told him to come in and shut the door. "You look upset. What's wrong?"

"Do you have any idea where Gilly might be? I've called her home and cell phones. She's got her voice mail turned on. When I went over to her house yesterday, she wasn't there. As far as I know she didn't come home last night.

"She wasn't there this morning when Jamal went over to talk to her. It's quarter to one and she's still not here. That's not like her. She cares for Jamal too much to miss this meeting. Frankly I'm worried tha—"

"Relax, Alex," he broke in. "I know where she went, and I have every confidence she'll be here by one."

Jim's response brought him up short. "Then you know a hell of a lot more than I do."

"If I were at liberty to tell you what's going on, I would."

Alex felt like he'd just taken a hit in the gut. "That sounds pretty ominous, Jim."

The other man studied him earnestly. "Knowing how your mind works, if you're imagining she's sick or something, let me assure you she's fine."

He swallowed hard. "You're a hundred percent sure of that?"

"I wouldn't lie to you."

"I know that." He closed his eyes for a moment. Something else was wrong. He'd felt so close to her the night they'd found Jamal at Island Park. But no matter how attracted she was to him, she kept distancing herself. The hope that she would tell him she'd changed her mind and wanted to go away with him was dimming fast.

"Alex?" He lifted his head, stunned to realize he'd been so deep in his thoughts, he'd almost forgotten Jim. "You look ill. Sit down for a minute."

"No. I'm all right."

But he wasn't all right and might never be again if Gilly continued to put him off.

Roberta poked her head in the door. "The superintendent just arrived with the governor."

Jim nodded to her. "We'll be there in a minute."

She shut the door again.

Letting out a troubled sigh Jim said, "I made a promise to Gilly, but you're in such bad shape, I'm beginning to think you've probably figured it out already."

Alex's heart began to thud. "Has she asked for a leave of absence?"

Jim's silence caused him to break out in a cold sweat. "Is she in California?"

When his friend didn't answer he said, "Never mind. I think you've just given me my answer."

As soon as Alex put Jamal on the plane in Salt Lake the day after tomorrow, he would catch one bound for San Diego. When he caught up to her, he'd get the whole truth out of her. No-holds-barred.

Gilly entered the noisy conference room with Sydney. All the same VIPs and head rangers were assembled. She and her friend slipped in and found some seats on the back row of chairs which had been set up for the overflow.

Jamal was seated at the table between Alex and Chief Archer. Steve Carr sat next to his father dressed in a suit. Jamal had dressed in his uniform like the rest of the rangers. Gilly thought he looked like one of the guys.

What a difference a month had made in Jamal's young life.

What a difference a month had made since Alex had come into *her* life.

She couldn't help her eyes from straying to his arresting profile, the set of his firm jaw and powerful shoulders. All that raw male charisma, the rugged masculinity that set him apart from the others made him the most beautiful man she'd ever known. It gave her tremendous pleasure to be able to look at him when he wasn't aware of it.

Soon Chief Archer stood up, causing the din to quiet down. She felt his gaze rest briefly on her as he scanned the room. He was probably wondering if she'd already accepted the job at Sequoia.

"I have to tell you that in all the time in my service as a ranger, I haven't known of a happier occasion than today. By now you've all heard the news that Jamal Carter and Steve Carr were instrumental in helping capture the sniper. It's made the national headlines.

"We're all indebted to you young men. As our way of honoring you, we'd like to present you with these plaques given by the park authority, and signed by the president of the United States. Your names are engraved. They say, 'In honor of meritorious service and courage.'"

He handed them to the boys. Gilly was so proud of Jamal, she probably clapped harder than anyone.

"The superintendent would like to say a few words."

Quinn Derek got to his feet and told Jamal to come up and stand by him. When he did his bidding, the older man said, "Jamal came to us as part of his high school careers program in Indianapolis.

"It was an experiment to see if he might find the life of a park ranger interesting enough to consider it for a career one day. In another day or two he has to fly home where his mother and sister are anxiously awaiting his return.

"From our end, the experiment turned out to be a success story greater than anyone could have imagined. Jamal's quick eye and intelligence saw something was wrong and helped avert what we all know was becoming a horrific situation.

"Earlier in the month he also had the presence of mind to pull Cindy Lewis out of harm's way at one of the thermal pools. In the process, his toes were scalded, but as we can all see, he has recovered. Jamal, you have the stuff heroes are made of. We salute you."

Quinn sounded all choked up.

"Now from your end, Jamal, what we want to know is, did you have a good time, not including the hospital visit? Was the experience worth it? Do you think other students would enjoy it? We'd all like to hear anything you have to say."

Jamal looked embarrassed and held on tightly to his award, but he had enough maturity to compose himself.

"It's been cool."

Gilly knew he was going to say that. While everyone laughed and clapped, tears welled up in her eyes.

"Ranger Latimer's the greatest." His wet brown eyes fastened on Alex. "I love you, man."

With those words, Gilly was dissolved and could just imagine how touched Alex was. The room went silent in recognition of the ultimate praise.

"But don't get mad if I tell you I don't want to be a ranger. I found out I want to go in the FBI."

At that revelation everyone in the room broke into cheers.

Agent Montoya got to his feet. "We'll be ready to welcome you into the department as soon as you finish your studies."

Jamal wiped his eyes. "Thanks, but I'm afraid that's not going to be for a while. I've got a problem with math. Ranger King's been helping me. I wish she were going to be my teacher when I get back to school."

Sydney pressed Gilly's arm.

"Since she's not here, I can tell you that even though she was nervous about the sniper, she and Alex came speeding to Island Park to help save me and Steve."

He shook his head. "She's so cool, and she makes the best doughnuts this side of the Continental Divide."

He'd picked that up from Alex.

Oh, Jamal.

The rangers on the back row looked over at her and grinned. Beth was in tears.

"I'm going to miss everybody."

The governor stood up. "I guess you got your answer, Quinn." He smiled at him, then Jamal. "We're going to follow your progress with great interest, son. When you're ready, I'll make my personal recommendation on your behalf for whatever field you choose to go into in life."

Jamal beamed. "Thanks." They shook hands.

While everyone clapped, the photographer took pictures. Soon Jamal was swamped by well-wishers.

Gilly got in line. As she stood waiting, her eyes trained on Alex who was over at the side talking with Quinn and the governor. While she was feasting her eyes on him, Alex happened to turn his head and their eyes connected. The impact set off an explosion of excitement that robbed her of breath.

He left the men and moved toward her as if he were following some invisible radar.

His gaze narrowed on her features. "How long have you been here?"

"Syd and I slipped in at the beginning." Her voice shook.

Shadows darkened his eyes. "Jamal was crushed when he thought you wouldn't be here today."

"I wouldn't have missed this for the world."

Lines bracketed his mouth. "Where have you been?"

"In California."

"Was there some kind of emergency?"

That was one way of putting it. "Yes."

His body stiffened. "But you're not going to tell me what it was because it's none of my business. No rangers allowed."

She felt his anger. It stunned her. "That's not it—"

"Then explain it to me," he demanded silkily.

"W-we can't talk here."

He inhaled harshly. "Name the time and the place! I'm free for the day."

"Aren't you planning to spend all of it with Jamal?"

"The kids have planned a going away party for him at Steve's house. His father won't be bringing him home until tonight. Since you're not on duty today, there's no time like the present."

She avoided his eyes. "I have to drive Syd back to Old Faithful."

"I'll follow you to her house."

"First I need to hug Jamal."

"In case you didn't notice, he's already gone."

When she looked around, she saw that it was true. She'd been so involved with Alex, she hadn't noticed anything else. Even Sydney had left the room. She presumed her friend was outside in the parking lot waiting for her.

"Don't worry. There's always tonight or to-morrow morning to say your goodbyes to him. Right now we have something to talk about that's been long overdue. Shall we go?"

Alex was in such a forbidding mood, he wouldn't tolerate any objections she might raise. They walked through the building and out the main doors into the sun. It was a hot day for the park.

The whole time he accompanied her, she was so conscious of his nearness she took the greatest care not to brush against his solid body with her arm.

When Sydney saw Gilly, she separated from some of the other rangers. They both reached her Toyota at the same time. In the periphery Gilly watched Alex get in his truck parked on the next row over. She was trembling by the time she got behind the wheel.

"What happened in there?"

"Alex wants to talk to me."

"Whew. I noticed."

She started up the car and drove out to the main road. "I don't want him to know I'm planning to move back to California, but I don't see how I can avoid telling him now."

"If you're not honest with him, then you're only prolonging the inevitable. He's the kind of man who'll come and find you wherever you are."

"You're right."

After a period of silence Sydney turned to her. "I already knew how Jamal felt about *you,* but for as long as you live, will you ever forget what he said to Alex?"

"No," Gilly answered with her heart in her throat. In fact Jamal had taken the words right out of her mouth.

"I've been thinking about your plans, Gilly, and I'm seriously considering going back to school myself."

"You're kidding!"

"No. I've been a teacher, an airline attendant, a ranger—but I'm still restless. Even if you weren't leaving, I think it's time I moved on, too. My destiny doesn't seem to be here even if Chip insists that it is."

"You haven't known Chip that long. Give it more time. Your situation isn't like mine."

Gilly's heart gave little death gasps every time she looked in the rearview mirror and saw Alex's truck bearing down on her.

After letting Sydney off at Old Faithful with a promise to call her the next day so they could talk about Chip some more, Gilly headed for Grant Village. When she turned in her driveway,

Alex pulled alongside her. He leaned across the seat and spoke to her from the open passenger's window.

"Would you be more comfortable talking in your house or mine?"

"Yours," she said after making a split-second decision. Once she'd told him the truth, then it would be on her terms when she left for hers. Alone.

CHAPTER TEN

ALEX drove on into the garage. Gilly walked up to his front porch and waited for him to open the door. For one week out of the month she'd spent a lot of time under his roof. But after tomorrow Jamal would be gone, and she wouldn't have an excuse to come over again.

"What would you like to drink?" he asked after inviting her in. "You kept my fridge so well stocked for all the visitors, I'm still loaded with drinks and treats."

She followed him into the kitchen "A cola sounds good."

He pulled two from the rack and handed her one.

Their knuckles brushed. Even that tiny contact sent a ripple of delight through her body. "Thank you," she murmured, pulling off the tab.

"It's cooler in the living room. Shall we go in there?"

Like her house, his came furnished with the same kind of generic furniture featuring a rustic flavor. She'd added knickknacks and small framed photos to hers to give it a little cozier feel.

Alex's living room was purely "male functional." He lived in his study and it reflected the kind of work he did with its charts and graphs. She hadn't seen his bedroom, but she imagined it wasn't much different than the living room.

All he needed was a place to hang his proverbial hat. After living in foster homes throughout his youth, she supposed the decor of a place didn't matter to him in the greater scheme of things. But she had to admit he was an excellent housekeeper. No matter when she came over, it was always clean and neat.

Since Kenny's death, Gilly hadn't been that driven to keep a perfect house. With no one to share it, she never saw the importance. Alex could run rings around her in that department. From what Jamal had told her, she knew for a fact Alex was a better cook.

"What are you thinking about so hard?"

Once again he stood in the middle of the room looking amazing in his uniform while she sat down on the end of the couch with one leg folded beneath her.

"If I paid you a compliment, you'd probably scoff."

He swallowed the rest of his drink and put the can on the coffee table. "Try me."

"I've been over here enough times to see that you'd make someone the perfect wife. Not a speck of dust, and everything in its place."

His eyes flickered. "I'll accept your compliment since it's only the second one you've ever given me."

She almost choked on her drink. "I didn't realize you were keeping score."

"It's the scientist in me. My job is to solve mysteries. So far you've presented one greater than the origin of the universe. I didn't think that was possible," he mocked.

There was no accompanying humor in his eyes. She started to get nervous.

"I know you're over Kenny. I know you're not frightened of intimacy. That's two out of three. Help me with the third one. What's going on?" His question reverberated in the room, penetrating her heart. "Why are you shutting me out when I know you want me as badly as I want you?" his voice grated.

Unable to sit there any longer, she got up from the couch. "I won't deny that I'm very attracted to you. But if I were to go away with you as you suggested, then what?"

His eyes blazed like silver fire. "Then we'd come back here after and contin—"

"Continue what?" she asked gently. "When we were at the hospital, you told me you could never be a father. So would we live together? Or were you thinking we'd just stay in our separate houses and run between the two when we felt the urge?

"That would be the perfect way to handle it, Alex. Then if you happened to meet another woman who pleased you, you wouldn't have to make any kind of explanation to me because in reality, you live alone. It's the ideal setup. I find no fault in it where you're concerned."

His features slowly hardened to take on a chiseled cast.

"But if you look at it from my standpoint, there's a lot wrong with it. I'm the ice princess if you remember. It's the image I've tried to promote because it's so hard to be a woman in this business.

"Once the rangers found out I was granting you favors I wasn't giving out to any of them, I'd be in for another kind of harassment. I can tell you now I'd be a marked woman, because a woman is held to a different standard. You can't deny it."

"I wasn't going to," he ground out.

"And then there's the problem of my getting pregnant, by accident of course. But there is no such thing as one hundred percent protection. I don't want to bring a child into the world without a loving father who'll give our baby his name.

"After seeing you with Jamal, I know you could do the loving part because you're a natural at it. But when he or she grows up, his or her friends would make judgments that could hurt them throughout their whole life.

"Worse would be if you decided you wanted to go live with someone else for a while. What would you say to them?

"Son? Little sweetheart? Don't worry. I still love you no matter where I am. You have to understand that sometimes your dad gets the urge to be with someone else. It's just the way I'm made. But I'll be around and available if you need me. Here's my cell phone number. I promise to come and visit you real soon."

Gilly realized she was going over the top with this, but she couldn't seem to stop what was pouring out of her.

"The problem with that scenario is that after you left, I would have to pick up the pieces. Unfortunately some of them would be too splintered to get up with my fingernails.

"In order to have any kind of a life, I'd probably have to give up my ranger job and move someplace where both my child and I would find more acceptance.

"It would mean going farther away from you, but that wouldn't cause you any grief to speak of because you'd make an effort to visit your child a couple of times a year and that would satisfy you."

He'd developed a noticeable pallor. "Don't say any more, Gilly."

"I have to. It's just one more thing. Then I'll leave. So far I've enjoyed our relationship more than you'll ever know. You've given me thrills I didn't expect to feel again. If we end it now, then we can both retain the beauty of what we shared while Jamal was in your care.

"Since I'm such a pushover where you're concerned, I've decided to be proactive about my attraction to you. That's why I've given my notice to Jim."

There was instant stillness.

"What are you saying?" he almost hissed the words.

"A few days ago I started looking for another job with the park service. Yesterday I interviewed for a position at Sequoia Park in California. I believe I could have it if I pushed for it. But on the way back here, I realized I don't want it after all.

"I'm going back to San Diego the day after tomorrow and see about getting myself enrolled in graduate school. That is if I pass the LSAT. My mom will think it's great. I think Trevor will feel the same, but at first it's going to blow his mind if I end up getting into law school.

"Much as I love it here, I'm afraid a certain brilliant volcanologist could probably talk me into doing something that would bring me joy now, but agony later on.

"I know what agony is like, and I don't want to suffer it again if I can help it. I realize no one knows what the future will bring, but if I leave the park now, I increase my chances of a happy life down the road.

"Your life will be happier, too. Look at it this way—you won't have to experience the guilt you will probably feel when your ardor cools and you have to come to me and explain that you aren't as enamored of me in the same way as you once were.

"It would be awful to have to tell anyone you'd been intimate with that the thrill was gone. I wouldn't want you to have to go through that. I wouldn't want to hear it. Nothing's worth that kind of pain."

She headed for the front door, terrified she might not make it to her house before she really lost it.

"If Jamal wants to see me tonight, tell him to come over. Otherwise I'll be over at six in the morning to say goodbye to him.

"I have to admit it'll be a wrench to see him go. He's worked his way into my heart. I bet his mom can't wait to hug her boy again. I know you're going to miss him, too," she whispered.

"What he said to you in front of your peer group is the kind of compliment you can't buy. Love has to be earned. It was such a powerful moment, every eye was wet. I still have gooseflesh.

"No one in that room will ever forget his tribute to you. It had to be the supreme highlight of your life, Alex Latimer."

She closed the door behind her and ran.

When Alex heard Bob's car in the driveway, he walked outside. A night wind had sprung up out of nowhere. There was going to be a storm before morning.

"Thanks for bringing Jamal home, Bob!"

"It was our pleasure."

Jamal climbed out of the car. "Thanks for the ride and the party, Mr. Carr. See you, Steve."

"Call me when you get back home."

"I will."

Alex watched the boys high-five each other before following Jamal into the house.

He took the plaque from his hand to examine it. "Not too many people in the whole world have received one of these. I guarantee no individual in the state of Indiana will have anything like it sitting on their dresser."

"I know." His voice lacked enthusiasm.

"Did I tell you they'll be sending you a framed picture showing you standing with the governor and the superintendent? Your mom's going to treasure that."

Alex expected some kind of response from him. They never ran out of things to talk about.

As he lifted his head in question, he was surprised to discover Jamal eyeing him with one of those glances that said he was only halfway listening to him.

"What?"

"Where's Gilly?"

He put the award down on the coffee table. "Home, I would imagine."

Jamal cocked his head. "I stay away all day to give you time with her and what happens? She's not even here. You don't look so good."

It was surprising how in one month Jamal had

gotten to know Alex so well he could read beneath the surface.

"I got a bit of a jolt today."

"What did she do? Go out on a date with one of the other rangers to make *you* jealous?"

"She doesn't have to do that to grab my attention."

"Well she's done something that makes you look the way I feel every time I smell those sulphur fumes."

Alex breathed in heavily. "She's leaving for California the day after tomorrow, and won't be returning."

"No way—"

"I'm afraid it's true. Jim confirmed it right before today's meeting."

"Then you've got to stop her."

"It's a career move. She's going back to college."

"That's crazy! She loves being a ranger."

He grimaced. "Not anymore."

"What did you do to her?"

If it had been anyone else who'd asked him that question in that particular way...

"I invited her to go away with me for a couple of weeks after I put you on the plane."

Jamal scratched his head. "And do what?"

"What do you think?"

"Oh, man—" He rolled his eyes.

"What?"

"You can get any woman to do that, but you don't ask someone like Gilly. You pop the big question first."

Alex had already found that out. Trust Jamal to have known it instinctively. As Larry had said, Jamal was born with certain smarts that couldn't be learned. He just came that way.

Jamal broke into a grin. "I didn't think anything could terrify you, but the big question scares the begeebers out of you doesn't it." He laughed so hard he slapped his leg.

"It's not funny."

"If you could see your face—"

"Wait till it happens to you one day."

"What's the big deal? The preacher does his job, then she moves in here, or you move in there. I admit she's no great cook, except for her doughnuts, but you could teach her."

"What if she doesn't love me?"

"Is Old Faithful still faithful?" Jamal had picked that up from Gilly. "Do you want me to run next door and ask her?"

"What do you think?" he muttered testily.

"I think you'd better get over there and do whatever you've got to do to stop her from leaving. But it's going to have to be good!" he warned.

"You mean get down on my knees?"

Jamal smiled. "Yeah. Now you're talking. What I'd give to see a sight like that!"

Alex raked both hands through his hair. "Will you be all right if I'm gone for a while?"

"Sure. I've got washing and packing to do."

"What if she won't let me in?"

"Leave it to me," Jamal said. "I'll call her and tell her I'm coming over. When she opens the door, wedge your foot so she can't slam it shut in your face."

"You think she's that upset?"

"Oh, yeah."

The one thing about Jamal. Alex had always been able to count on was his honesty. "That's a good idea."

"When you get to the good part, tell her it's forever. Women love to hear stuff like that."

"How many women have you told that to? Come clean now."

"I'm waiting for the right one. Some day I'm going to find me one as cool as Gilly. Like Larry said when he found out you were living next door to her, you're a lucky dog."

While Gilly was packing up all her painting supplies, her cell phone rang. The caller ID indicated it was coming from next door. Since she'd seen Ranger Carr's Honda in Alex's driveway earlier, she imagined it was Jamal phoning.

She was glad. For the last few nights she'd been doing a flower painting for him to take home to his mom. It was like the one she'd done for her own mom.

Gilly would rather give it to him tonight and hug him goodbye in private. After the things she'd said to Alex earlier, she couldn't face him right now.

She reached for the phone on the kitchen wall and picked up. "Hello?"

"Hi, Gilly."

"Hi yourself, Jamal. How was the party?"

"I think I ate too much cake."

"You only think?"

"It was pretty good. Is it okay if I come over for a few minutes?"

She was already feeling the wrench of separation. "Of course. Today you left the meeting before I got a chance to congratulate you."

"You were there?" he asked in surprise.

"Would I lie to you?"

"Did I make you mad when I told everybody you were kind of nervous about the sniper?"

"No," she answered honestly. "The rangers think I'm made of ice. Now they know differently." Not that it mattered. Day after tomorrow she'd be gone. "Come on over."

"Okay."

She hung up the phone. When she reached the front door and opened it, she got the shock of her life to see Alex standing there. Jamal was nowhere in sight. She actually felt faint.

Before she could think or speak, he stepped past her and closed it. "We have to talk."

Her breathing grew shallow. "We already did that earlier."

"As I recall, you were the one who did most of it. I just listened. Now it's your turn to hear me out."

She rushed past him to the kitchen, needing to keep busy so he couldn't tell how his presence had completely thrown her.

For a few minutes he said nothing and only stood there watching while she packed her brushes and tubes of paint in the box

"I forgot to add one thing when I asked you to go away with me."

"What was that?" she kept working.

"I'm in love with you."

"No you're not," Gilly flung the declaration back at him and reached for more supplies to pack.

"Did you hear what I just said?"

"Yes. All it means is that you've been carried away by the heat of the moment. I can relate. But if you think that's going to help me change my mind, then you simply don't get it, brilliant as you are."

"Then what *would* work?"

She shook her head, unable to say anything because her pain was too great.

"I'll need special help if I'm going to be your husband."

Husband?

Gilly's legs started to shake.

"The thought of marriage has always terrified me. I never felt it was for someone coming from my background. There were a lot of things I figured I'd fail at in life, but I didn't want that to be one of them, so I grew up circumnavigating the very possibility.

"Marriage is too important. I didn't see many good marriages growing up in those foster homes, and I know what it did to me to be born an unwanted appendage of a mother who couldn't remember which man she slept with to produce me. Theirs wasn't a union sanctified in the bonds of holy matrimony.

"Unfortunately my anger was so raw over the way I came into the world, I didn't want any part of it. Since college I've seen couples marry, then heard about their divorces a few years later. Every time the bad news reached me, I congratulated myself on my escape.

"But that was before I was transferred here and fell in love with a certain female ranger. I saw you as a challenge to overcome because, like me, I sensed you'd been hardened by something in your life, too. I just didn't know who did it to you, or why.

"The more you kept your distance from me, the more determined I was to outmaneuver you until I broke you down. Every time I thought I was getting closer to success, you said or did something that threw my world into further chaos.

"But the thought of you leaving me and never coming back made my worst nightmare pale in comparison."

She couldn't believe this was coming out of him.

"You can't go, Gilly. I need you too much. Since it's the only way I can have you at my side, waking and sleeping for the rest of our lives, you've got to marry me!"

He gripped her shoulders hard, not knowing his own strength. "Do you hear me? I didn't mean what I said at the hospital. We'll work together and we'll have it all. The house, the children, the dancing and karate lessons you told Jamal about when you were discussing your dreams.

"I long to meet your family and become a part of them. I ache for that kind of closeness with legitimate family. It's something I've missed my whole life. The thought of in-laws, parents—the people who love you and reared you. I want to get to know them. I want our children to play with your brothers' children.

"Having Jamal live with me has given me a taste of things I crave. But it's not enough. Not nearly enough. Since I saw you at Grandy's standing there in the sun, the ultimate picture of the perfect woman for me, I want it all. With you I can see it all."

When she stared into his eyes, she saw everything she hadn't seen earlier. All the secrets he'd kept hidden from her. This strong, incredible man, whose psyche was as fragile as Jamal's, had just laid his soul bare to her.

"I'll do whatever it takes to make it work," he whispered feverishly. "I swear I'll love you forever. You're the one and only love of my life, Gilly King. With you I could be something better than I am.

"Will you take a chance on this old bachelor

and be my wife? If you're at my side, I feel like I can do anything."

The pleading in those gorgeous gray eyes was so humbling, and filled her heart with so much joy, she couldn't contain it.

She slid her hands up his chest and around his neck, crying out his name. "It's what I want with every fiber of my being. I was afraid I'd never hear those words from you. It seems like I've always loved you even though it's only been a month.

"Don't you know it's because I'm so in love with you that I couldn't bear to stay here any longer? I'm one woman who has to have the whole loaf. Anything less would crucify me."

In the next breath she was covering his face with kisses, trying to show him, trying to tell him he was her whole life! Their mouths clung in rapture until they were both weaving in place from the depth of their passion.

Gilly didn't have to hold back her feelings any longer. Alex wanted to marry her. Entwined in his arms, she was so swept away by her emotions, she was on fire for him and barely coherent.

"When do you want to get married, darling? Now that I know you love me, I'll agree to whatever you say, but I'm telling you now I'm not a patient man."

"I have no patience where you're concerned, either," she admitted, kissing him with abandon. "Tomorrow's the Fourth of July. How about the end of August? That ought to be enough time for my family to help us plan a wedding. I can't wait to show you off. They're going to be so impressed with you. And after they really get to know you, they'll love you to death the way I do."

He gave her another kiss so enthralling it barely registered that the doorbell had rung.

Alex made a noise in his throat, then pressed his forehead to hers. "That'll be Jamal checking on us. He's dying to know if I popped the question."

Gilly loved that boy. "We have to let him in."

She was still reeling from another kiss when he called out to Jamal that they were in the living room. By the time he came inside, Alex had grabbed her around the waist from behind, holding her so close there was no air between them.

"Jamal Carter? Be the first to say hello to the future Mrs. Latimer. I don't have a ring for her yet, but take it from me. It's official."

Jamal stood there grinning like a Cheshire cat. He stared at Alex. "Did you get down on your knees?"

"Yes—" she answered before Alex could say

anything. He'd laid himself down; his knees, his heart, his soul. For as long as she lived, Gilly would never forget his proposal or the fact that he'd made her feel immortal.

"When's the wedding?"

"Next month," Alex informed him.

"Where?"

"Del Mar. You'll have to come since you're going to be my best man, right?"

He blinked. "Me?"

"No one else. We'll pick out our tuxedos together."

"I love a man in a black tuxedo as much as one in uniform." She winked at Alex. "You guys will look spectacular."

"Yeah?" Jamal sounded pretty excited about that.

"Maybe this time we can talk your mom and sister into coming, too," Alex said.

"That would be cool. Which house are you two going to live in?

Gilly turned in her new fiancé's arms. She would never tire of staring at the handsome man who'd just made her the happiest woman alive.

"Probably yours. It would be a nightmare to take your study apart and then try to put it back together again over here in precisely the same order."

His eyes narrowed on her mouth. "I didn't know you were familiar with my study."

"There's a lot of stuff you don't know," Jamal quipped.

"Jamal—" she protested, hot faced.

He laughed all the way out the front door.

Alex's eyes were alive with desire. "What kind of information has Jamal been keeping from me? Come on, tell me or I'll have to start tickling you."

"No—" she screamed and started running away from him. But he was too fast for her. One arm snaked around her body. He crushed her to him.

"Please don't tickle me, darling— I can't stand it."

His deep laugh resonated to her insides. He kissed the side of her neck. "I'll show mercy if you tell me what I want to know."

They were both breathing hard. "He must have overheard me talking to Syd about something while I thought he was asleep."

"When?"

"I don't know. We had several conversations."

"About what?"

"A-about what I would do with your house if I had the right to fix it up. Besides some decorating ideas, I may have mentioned that the middle room would make the perfect-size nursery."

"*May* have? What else?" he asked with an intensity that shook her to the very essence of her being.

"I think I might have said something about…learning how to cook so I could keep you…enslaved?"

A tremor ran through his powerful body she could feel. He kissed both sides of her mouth. "You already do that by just being you," his voice throbbed before he began plundering her mouth as if it were the breath of life to him.

"Gilly—" he cried. His fingers tangled her hair. "Tell me I'm not dreaming, darling. I couldn't take it. Not now. I don't ever want to experience the emptiness I felt when you told me you were going back to California for good."

She kissed his mouth feverishly. "I felt that same desolation while I was at Sequoia Park. I thought 'Where can I run? Where can I go where I won't be haunted by you?' I was only kidding myself that I could push you away by studying hard. It wouldn't have worked.

"You mean everything to me, Alex. Do you know I've been envious of Jamal?"

"Gilly—"

"It's true. He had an entrée to your affections. I would have given anything to trade places with him in that hospital bed. I wanted to feel all that love you had to give, poured out on me.

"The night we were at the restaurant and the lights went out, you made us feel safe. I found myself wanting to be in your presence every second.

"When you arrested that construction worker outside the bar, I almost threw my arms around you in front of everyone. It's a miracle I was able to contain myself.

"Oh, darling, just hold me for a little, while it sinks in that you want to be my husband."

He crushed her against him. "Let me give Jim a quick call to tell him he's not losing the park's poster ranger, then I'm all yours."

She needed to e-mail Chief Ranger Meeks, too, but before she did that, she caught his hard-planed cheeks in her hands. "What do you mean 'poster ranger'?"

Alex flashed her a white smile. "When I first asked him about you, he told me he'd purposely placed you at West Thumb. That's because you're the epitome of the perfect female ranger, and the park's most beautiful attraction.

"I happen to know he hated the thought of losing you. So far he hasn't found anyone who can touch you, let alone take your place. He'll be overjoyed at our news."

"*Alex—*"

"That was a compliment, darling." He swooped down to give her another long, hard kiss.

"It's no secret that every unattached male is in love with you. I can't wait to send out our wedding announcements. When they find out that Smoky the Bear has raided camp and stolen the prized goody, you'll hear mass howling from one end to the other of both parks."

She buried her face in his neck, still in a daze that he wanted to marry her.

"Jim will probably have to declare a week of mourning while the poor devils deal with the fact that the ice princess from number eleven is in permanent meltdown with Dr. Latimer of the Volcano Observatory at number ten."

Permanent meltdown was right.

And it was getting hotter by the second.

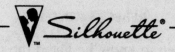

SPECIAL EDITION™

Emotional, compelling stories that capture the intensity of living, loving and creating a family in today's world.

Desire

Modern, passionate reads that are powerful and provocative.

INTIMATE MOMENTS™

Romances that are sparked by danger and fueled by passion.

SILHOUETTE Romance

From today to forever, these love stories offer today's woman fairytale romance.

BOMBSHELL

Action-filled romances with strong, sexy, savvy women who save the day.

SILHOUETTE *Romance*

Escape to a place where a kiss is still a kiss...

Feel the breathless connection...

Fall in love as though it were the very first time...

Experience the power of love!

Come to where favorite authors—such as

Diana Palmer, Stella Bagwell, Marie Ferrarella

and many more—deliver modern fairy tale romances and genuine emotion, time after time after time....

Silhouette Romance— from today to forever.

Silhouette®

Live the possibilities

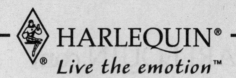